THE
BUNKER
DIARY

Carolrhoda Lab™
An imprint of Carolrhoda Books
A division of Lerner Publishing Group, Inc.
241 First Avenue North
Minneapolis, MN 55401 USA

For reading levels and more information, look up this title at
www.lernerbooks.com.

Cover photo © Getty. Cover design by samcombes.co.uk.

Main body text set in Sabon LT Std 10/14.
Typeface provided by Adobe Systems.

Library of Congress Cataloging-in-Publication Data

Brooks, Kevin.
    The bunker diary / by Kevin Brooks.
        pages   cm — (The Bunker Diary)
    "First published in 2013 by Penguin Books Ltd, 80 Strand,
London WC2R 0RL, England."
    ISBN 978-1-4677-5420-0 (trade hard cover : alk. paper)
    ISBN 978-1-4677-7646-2 (EB pdf)
    [1. Kidnapping—Fiction. 2. Interpersonal relations—Fiction. 3.
Torture—Fiction. 4. Conduct of life—Fiction. 5. Diaries—Fiction.]
I. Title.
PZ7.B7965Bun 2015
[Fic]—dc23   2014026362

Manufactured in the United States of America
2 – SB – 6/15/15

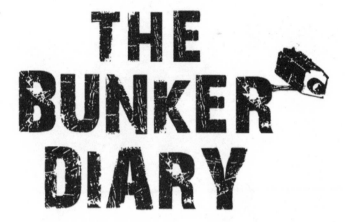

THE BUNKER DIARY

KEVIN BROOKS

🌿 carolrhoda LAB
MINNEAPOLIS

Monday, 30 January

10:00 a.m.

This is what I know. I'm in a low-ceilinged rectangular building made entirely of whitewashed concrete. It's about twelve metres wide and eighteen metres long. A corridor runs down the middle of the building, with a smaller corridor leading off to a lift shaft just over halfway down. There are six little rooms along the main corridor, three on either side. They're all the same size, three metres by five, and each one is furnished with an iron-framed bed, a hard-backed chair, and a bedside cabinet. There's a bathroom at one end of the corridor and a kitchen at the other. Opposite the kitchen, in the middle of an open area, there's a rectangular wooden table with six wooden chairs. In each corner of the open area there's an L-shaped bench settee.

There are no windows. No doors. The lift is the only way in or out.

The whole place looks something like this:

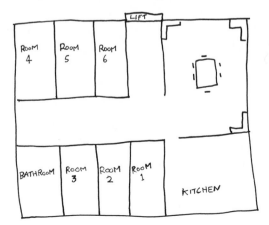

In the bathroom there's a steel bathtub, a steel sink, and a steel toilet. No mirrors, no cupboards, no accessories. The kitchen contains a sink, a table, some chairs, an electric cooker, a small fridge, and a wall-mounted cupboard. In the cupboard there's a plastic washing-up bowl, six plastic dinner plates, six plastic glasses, six plastic mugs, six sets of plastic cutlery.

Why six?

I don't know.

I'm the only one here.

It feels underground in here. The air is heavy, concrete, damp. It's *not* damp, it just feels damp. And it smells like a place that's old, but new. Like it's been here a long time but never been used.

There are no light switches anywhere.

There's a clock on the corridor wall.

The lights come on at eight o'clock in the morning, and they go off again at midnight.

There's a low humming sound deep within the walls.

12:15 p.m.

Nothing moves.

Time is slow.

I thought he was blind. That's how he got me. I still can't believe I fell for it. I keep playing it over in my mind, hoping I'll do something different, but it always turns out the same.

It was early Sunday morning when it happened. Yesterday morning. I wasn't doing anything in particular, just hanging around the concourse at Liverpool Street station, trying to keep warm, looking out for Saturday night leftovers. I had my hands in my pockets, my guitar on my back, my eyes to the ground. Sunday morning is a good time for finding things. People get drunk on Saturday night. They rush to get the last train home. They drop stuff. Cash, cards, hats, gloves, cigarettes. The cleaners get most of the good stuff, but sometimes they miss things. I found a fake Rolex once. Got a tenner for it. So it's always worth looking. But all I'd found that morning was a broken umbrella and a half-empty packet of Marlboros. I threw the umbrella away but kept the cigarettes. I don't smoke, but cigarettes are always worth keeping.

So there I was, just hanging around, minding my own business, when a couple of platform staff came out of a side door and started walking towards me. One of them was a regular, a young black guy called Buddy who's usually OK, but I didn't know the other one. And I didn't like the look of him. He was a big guy in a peaked cap and steel-tipped shoes, and he looked like trouble. He probably wasn't, and they probably wouldn't have bothered me anyway, but it's always best to play safe, so I put my head down, pulled up my hood, and moved off towards the taxi rank.

And that's when I saw him. The blind man. Raincoat, hat, dark glasses, white stick. He was standing at the back of a dark-coloured van. A Ford Transit, I think. The back doors were open and there was a heavy-looking suitcase on the ground. The blind man was struggling to get the case in the back of the van. He wasn't having much luck. There was something wrong with his arm. It was in a sling.

It was still pretty early and the station was deserted. I could hear the two platform men jangling their keys and laughing about something, and from the sound of the big guy's clackety-clack footsteps I could tell they were moving away from me, heading off towards the escalator that leads up to McDonald's. I waited a little while just to make sure they weren't coming back, then I turned my attention to the blind man. Apart from the Transit van, the taxi rank was empty. No black cabs, no one waiting. There was just me and this blind man. A blind man with his arm in a sling.

I thought about it.

You could walk away if you wanted to, I told myself. You don't have to help him. You could just walk away, nice and quiet. He's blind, he'll never know, will he?

But I didn't walk away.

I'm a nice guy.

I coughed to let him know I was there, then I walked up and asked him if he needed any help. He didn't look at me. He kept his head down. And I thought that was a bit odd. But then I thought, maybe that's what blind people do? I mean, what's the point of looking at someone if you can't actually see them?

"It's my arm," he muttered, indicating the sling. "I can't get hold of the suitcase properly."

I bent down and picked it up. It wasn't as heavy as it looked.

"Where do you want it?" I asked.

"In the back," he said. "Thank you."

There was no one else in the van, no one in the driving seat. Which was kind of surprising. The back of the van was pretty empty too, just a few bits of rope, some shopping bags, a dusty old blanket.

The blind man said, "Would you mind putting the case up by the front seats for me? It'll be easier to get out."

I was beginning to feel a bit uneasy now. Something didn't

4

feel right. What was this guy doing here? Where was he going? Where had he been? Why was he all alone? How the hell could he drive? I mean, a blind man with a broken arm?

"If you wouldn't mind?" he said.

Maybe he isn't completely blind? I thought. Maybe he can see enough to drive? Or maybe he's one of those people who pretend they're disabled so they can get a special parking badge?

"Please," he said. "I'm in a hurry."

I shrugged off my doubts and stepped up into the van. What did I care if he was blind or not? Just get his suitcase into the van and leave him to it. Go and find somewhere warm. Wait for the day to get going. See who's around—Lugless, Pretty Bob, Windsor Jack. See what's happening.

I was moving towards the front seats when I felt the van lurch on its springs, and I knew the blind man had climbed up behind me.

"I'll show you where to put it," he said.

I knew I'd been had then, but it was already too late, and as I turned to face him he grabbed my head and clamped a damp cloth over my face. I started to choke. I was breathing in chemicals—chloroform, ether, whatever it was. I couldn't breathe. There was no air. My lungs were on fire. I thought I was dying. I struggled, lashing out with my elbows and legs, kicking, stamping, jerking my head like a madman, but it was no good. He was strong, a lot stronger than he looked. His hands gripped my skull like a couple of vices. After a few seconds I started to feel dizzy, and then . . .

Nothing.

I must have passed out.

The next thing I knew I was sitting in a wheelchair inside a large metal box. My head was all mushy and I was only half awake, and for a moment or two I genuinely thought I was dead. All I could see in front of me was a receding tunnel of harsh white light. I thought it was the tunnel of death. I thought I was buried in a metal coffin.

When it finally dawned on me that I wasn't dead, that it wasn't a coffin, that the large metal box was in fact just a lift, and that the lift door was open, and the tunnel of death was nothing more than a plain white corridor stretching out in front of me, I was so relieved that for a few short seconds I actually felt like laughing.

The feeling didn't last long.

After I'd got up out of the wheelchair and stumbled into the corridor, I'm not sure what happened for a while. Maybe I passed out again—I don't know. All I can really remember is the lift door closing and the lift going up.

I don't think it went very far.

I heard it stop—*g-dung, g-dunk*.

It was nine o'clock at night now. I was still sick and dopey, and I kept burping up a horrible taste of gassy chemicals. I was scared to death. Shocked. Shaking. Totally confused. I didn't know what to do.

I went into one of the rooms and sat down on the bed.

Three hours later, at twelve o'clock precisely, the lights went off.

I sat there for a while in the petrified darkness, listening hard for the sound of the lift coming back down. I don't know what

I was expecting, a miracle maybe, or perhaps a nightmare. But nothing happened. No lift, no footsteps. No cavalry, no monsters. Nothing.

The place was as dead as a graveyard.

I thought the blind man might be waiting for me to fall asleep, but there was no chance of that. I was wide awake. And my eyes were staying open.

But I suppose I must have been more tired than I thought. Either that or I was still suffering from whatever he drugged me with. Probably a bit of both.

I don't know what time it was when I finally fell asleep.

It was still dark when I woke up this morning. I didn't have any of that "where am I?" feeling you're supposed to get when you wake up in a strange place. As soon as my eyes opened I knew where I was. I still didn't know *where* I was, of course, but I knew it was the same unknown darkness I'd gone to sleep in. I recognized the underground feel of the air.

The room was blacker than anything. Lightless. Sightless. I groped my way to the door and went out into the corridor, but that was no better. Dark as hell. I couldn't tell if my eyes were open or shut. Couldn't see a thing. Didn't know what time it was. Couldn't see the clock. Couldn't even guess what time it was. There's nothing to guess from. No windows, no view, no sky, no sounds. Just solid darkness and that unnerving low humming in the walls.

I felt like nothing. Existing in nothing.

Black all over.

I kept touching the walls and tapping my foot on the floor to convince myself that I was real.

I had to go to the bathroom.

I was about halfway along the corridor, feeling my way along the wall, when all of a sudden the lights came on. *Blam!* A silent flash, and the whole place was lit up in a blaze of sterile white. Scared the life out of me. I couldn't move for a good five minutes. I just stood there with my back against the wall, trying hard not to wet myself.

The clock on the wall was ticking.

Tick tock, tick tock.

And my eyes were drawn to it. It seemed really important to know what time it was, to see movement. It somehow seemed to mean something to me. A sign of life, I suppose. Something to rely on.

It was five past eight.

I went to the bathroom.

At nine o'clock, the lift came back down again.

I was poking around in the kitchen at the time, trying to find something to use as a weapon, something sharp, or heavy, or sharp *and* heavy. No luck. Everything is either bolted down, welded to the wall, or made of plastic. I was looking inside the cooker, wondering if I could rip out some bits of metal or something, when I heard the lift starting up—*g-dung, g-dunk*, a heavy whirring noise, a solid *clunk*, a sharp *click* . . .

And then the sound of the lift coming down—*nnnnnnnnnn* . . .

I grabbed a plastic fork and went out into the corridor. The lift door was shut but I could hear the lift getting closer—*nnnnnnnnnnnn* . . .

My muscles tensed. My fingers gripped the plastic fork. It felt pathetic, useless. The lift stopped. *G-dunk*. I snapped the end off the fork, rubbed the jagged end with my thumb and watched as the lift door opened—*mmm-kshhh-tkk*.

Nothing.

It was empty.

When I was a little kid I used to have recurring dreams about a lift. The dream took place in a big tower block in the middle of town, right next to a roundabout. I didn't know what the building was. Flats, an office building, something like that. I didn't know what town it was either. It wasn't my town, I knew that. It was a big place, kind of grey, with lots of tall buildings and wide grey streets. A bit like London. But it wasn't London. It was just a town. A dream town.

In my dream I'd go into the tower block and wait for the lift, watching the lights, and when the lift came down I'd step inside, the door would close, and I'd suddenly realize that I didn't know where I was going. I didn't know which floor I wanted. Which button to press. I didn't know anything. The lift would start up, get moving, and then the dream-panic would set in. Where am I going? What am I going to do? Should I press a button? Should I shout for help?

I can't remember anything else about it.

This morning, when the lift came down and the door slid open, I kept my distance for a while, just standing well back and staring at it. I don't know what I was waiting for. Just to see if anything happened, I suppose. But nothing did. Eventually, after about ten minutes or so, I cautiously moved closer and looked inside. I didn't actually go inside, I just stood by the open door and looked around. There wasn't much to see. No controls. No buttons, no lights. No hatchway in the ceiling. Nothing but a clear plastic leaflet-holder screwed into the far wall. Plexiglass, letter size. Empty.

There's a matching leaflet-holder fixed to the corridor wall outside the lift. This one's filled with blank sheets of paper, and there's a ballpoint pen clipped to the wall beside it.

???

It's nearly midnight now. I've been here for nearly forty hours. Is that right? I think so. Anyway, I've been here a long time and nothing has happened. I'm still here. Still alive. Still staring at the walls. Writing these words. Thinking.

A thousand questions have streamed through my head.

Where am I?

Where's the blind man?

Who is he?

What does he want?

What's he going to do to me?

What am I going to do?

I don't know.

All right, what *do* I know?

I know I haven't been hurt. I'm all in one piece. Legs, arms, feet, hands. Everything's in working order.

I know I'm hungry.

And frightened.

And confused.

And angry.

My pockets have been emptied. I'd had a £10 note hidden away in one of my socks, and now it's gone. He must have searched me.

Bastard.

I think he knows who I am. God knows how, but he must do. It's the only thing that makes sense. He knows I'm Charlie Weems's son, he knows my dad's stinking rich, he's taken me for the money. Kidnapped me. That's what it is. A kidnapping. He's probably been in touch with Dad already. Rung him up. Got his number from somewhere, rung him up and demanded a ransom. Half a million in used notes in a black leather suitcase, drop it off at a motorway service station. No police or he'll cut my ears off.

Yeah, that's it. It has to be.

A straightforward kidnapping.

Dad's probably speeding down the motorway right now, whacked out of his head on brandy and dope, tired and grouchy, pissed off with me for costing him big again. I can just see his face, all scrunched up, his bloodshot eyes squinting through the windscreen at the glare of motorway lights, muttering madly to himself. Yeah, I can see him. He's probably wondering if he should have tried bargaining for me, offered 150K, settled for 300.

First thing he'll say when he gets me back is, "Where the hell have you been for the last five months? I've been worried stupid."

The lights have gone out.

8:15 a.m.

Day three.

I haven't eaten since Saturday.

I'm *starving*.

Why isn't he feeding me? What's the matter with him? Why doesn't he show himself? Why doesn't he threaten me, get tough, tell me to shut up, do as you're told and you won't get hurt . . . why doesn't he *do* something? *Any*thing.

Why am I still here?

Where's Dad?

I'm beginning to think he's refused to pay the ransom. That'd be just like Dad. I can just imagine him thinking it's all a joke, or a set-up. That I've kidnapped myself. Yeah, that's it. Mixed-up rich kid with semi-famous father, desperate for attention, sets up his own kidnapping to put one over on his dad.

Shit.

I'm *so* hungry.

There's a bible in the bedside cabinet. Last night I got so bored I picked it up and started leafing through it. Then I realized that I wasn't *that* bored, and I put it back in the drawer.

Each room has one. I've checked. Bible in the top drawer, blank notebook and pen in the middle. *This* notebook, *this* pen.

The drawers have locks and there's a little key on the top of each cabinet. Six keys, six notebooks, six pens, six rooms, six plates . . .

Six?

No, I haven't worked it out yet.

The notebooks are good quality—black-leather covers, fresh white pages. Blank pages. Lots of blank pages. I don't know why, but that bothers me.

The pen's a Uni-ball Eye, Micro, black. Waterproof/fade-proof. Made by the Mitsubishi Pencil Co. Ltd.

Just in case you're interested.

It's quarter to nine now.

The lights have been on for forty-five minutes.

Last night I spent some time sharpening the broken plastic fork. I only had my fingernails and teeth to work with, but I think I did a pretty good job. It doesn't look like much, and I don't think I could kill anyone with it, but it's sharp enough to do some damage.

If I'm right, the lift will come down in five minutes.

It did. Only this time it wasn't empty.

There was a little girl in there.

When I first saw her, my heart iced over and my brain went numb. I couldn't move, couldn't think, couldn't speak, couldn't do anything. It was too much to take in. She was sitting in the wheelchair, the same wheelchair I'd arrived in, kind of slumped to one side, with her eyes closed and her mouth half open. Her hair was all messed up and knotted, and her clothes were crumpled and covered in dust. Tear stains darkened her cheeks.

I didn't know what to do. Didn't know what to feel. Didn't know anything. All I could do was stand there with the sharpened plastic fork in my hand, staring like an idiot at this poor little girl.

Then my heart grew hot and a rage of emotions welled up inside me. Anger, pity, fear, panic, hatred, confusion, despair, sadness, madness. And I wanted to scream and shout and tear the walls down. I wanted to hit something, hit someone. Hit *him*. How could he *do* this? How could *anyone* do this? She's just a girl, for God's sake. She's just a *little girl*.

I closed my eyes, took a deep breath, and let it out slowly.

Think, I told myself.

Think.

I opened my eyes and studied the girl, looking for signs of life. Her eyes were still closed, her lips not moving.

Breathe . . . please breathe.

I waited, watching.

After a long ten seconds or so, her head twitched, she gave a little gulp, and her eyes fluttered open. I shook the paralysis from my body, hurried over to the lift, and wheeled her out.

Her name's Jenny Lane. She's nine years old. She was on her way to school this morning when a policeman stopped her in the street and told her that her mum had been in an accident.

"How did you know he was a policeman?" I asked her.

"He had a uniform and a hat. He showed me his badge. He said he'd take me to the hospital."

14

She started crying again then. She was in a terrible state. Streaming tears, shocked eyes, shaking like a leaf. She had a slight graze on her lip, and her knee was cut and bruised. Worst of all, she was breathing really fast. Short, sharp, gaspy little breaths. It was scary. I felt completely helpless. I don't know what you're supposed to do with little girls in shock. I just don't *know* stuff like that.

After I'd got her out of the lift, I took her to the bathroom and waited outside while she got herself cleaned up. Then I got her a drink of water and took her back to my room and tried to make her comfortable. It was the best I could do. Settle her down. Comfort her. Talk to her. Give her a smile. Ask her if she was all right.

"Are you all right?"

She sniffed and nodded.

"Are you hurt?"

She shook her head. "My tummy feels funny."

"Did he put a cloth over your mouth?"

She nodded again.

"What about your knee?"

"I knocked it. It's all right."

"Did he . . . ?"

"What?"

"Did he . . . ? " I coughed to cover my embarrassment. "Did he touch you or anything?"

"No." She wiped her nose. "Where is he?"

"I don't know. Upstairs somewhere."

"What's upstairs?"

"I don't know."

"Who is he?"

"I don't know."

"What's he called?"

"I don't know."

"Is he coming down here?"

"I don't think so."

She looked around. "What is this place? Do you live here?"

"No, the man brought me here."

"What for?"

"I don't know."

Don't know, don't know, don't know . . . probably not the most comforting answers in the world, but at least she wasn't crying any more. Her breathing was beginning to improve too.

I asked her where she lived.

"1 Harvey Close," she said.

I smiled. "Where? What town?"

"Moulton."

"Moulton in Essex?"

"Yes."

I nodded, then nodded again, trying to think of something else to say. I'm not that good at small talk. I don't know what you're supposed to say to nine-year-old girls.

I said, "What time was it when the policeman stopped you?"

"About half past seven."

"Isn't that a bit early for school?"

"We were going on a trip to the nucular power station."

"Nu*clear*."

"What?

"Nothing. Is that why you're not wearing school uniform, because you were going on a school trip?"

"Uh-huh."

She was wearing a little red jacket, a T-shirt, jeans, and trainers. There was a picture of a tiger on her T-shirt.

"What's your name?" she asked me.

"Linus."

"What?"

"Linus," I repeated, as I almost always have to. "Lye-nus."

"That's a funny name."

I smiled. "Yeah, I know."

"Is there anything to eat, Lye-nus?"

"Not at the moment."

I looked down at the trainers on her feet. Newish but cheap. Stuck-on stripes. Frayed laces.

I said, "What do your mum and dad do, Jenny?"

"Why?"

"I was just wondering, that's all."

She pulled at some knots in her hair. "Dad works at Costco. He doesn't like it much."

"What about your mum?"

She shrugged. "She's my mum."

"Does she work?"

She shook her head. "Nuh-uh."

"You're not rich, then?"

Her face creased into a frown. "Rich?"

"Forget it. Here." I passed her my hooded jacket. The room wasn't cold, but she was starting to shiver again and her face was really pale. "Put it on, it'll keep you warm."

So, no kidnapping then. Not for the money anyway. He's not going to get much of a ransom from a guy who works at Costco, is he? And besides, if he knows who I am, why bother kidnapping anyone else? I mean, you don't rob a bank and then stop on the way out to break into a bubblegum machine, do you? Not unless you're an idiot.

There's no point. No reason.

No kidnap.

Which means . . .

What?

I have to get out of here, that's what it means.

We have to get out of here.

The trouble is, I can't see how. Everything is solid concrete. The walls, the floor, the ceiling. The only way out is the lift. But that's hopeless. When the lift comes down the door stays open. When the lift goes up the door closes. The door is solid metal. Very thick. And the lift itself looks indestructible. And even if I could get through the door when the lift is up, what then? I don't know what's behind it. I don't how high the lift shaft is. It could be thirty metres of sheer concrete for all I know.

And anyway, he's watching us.

This afternoon, while Jenny was sleeping, I had another look round. A *really* good look round. Walking about, checking this, checking that, poking around, kicking walls, stamping on the floor.

It's hopeless.

It's like trying to escape from a sealed box.

After a while, I sat down at the dining table and stared at the ceiling. I couldn't help thinking of him up there. What's he doing? Is he sitting down, standing up, walking about? Is he laughing? Grinning? Picking his nose? What's he doing? Who is he? What? Who? Why?

Who are you?

What do you want?

What's your *kick*?

What's your *thing*?

And it was then, just as all these questions were floating around in my head, that I suddenly realized what I was staring at. There was a small circular grille set in the ceiling, directly above the dining table. I'd been looking at it for the last few minutes, but my eyes hadn't taken it in. A small circular grille, about 10 centimetres in diameter, made of white metal mesh, fixed flush to the ceiling. I stared hard, making sure I wasn't imagining it, and then I looked round and saw more of them. One, two, three, four. Four of them, spread out evenly along the length of the corridor.

I got up and checked the rest of the rooms.

The grilles are everywhere. There's one in the lift, one in the kitchen, one in the bathroom, one in each of the other rooms.

I went back and got up on the table for a closer look.

Each grille is a perfect circle, split in two. A faint breeze of warmish air comes out of one side, and an equally faint current is sucked in the other. Ventilation, I suppose.

Heating.

But there's more.

On either side of the grille there's a little hole cut in the mesh. Embedded in each of the holes are two little buggy things. One is a flat silver disc about the size of a 5p coin, the other is like a small white bead with a tiny glass eye at the end.

Like this.

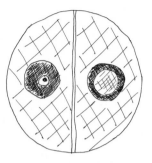

Microphone.
Camera.
Shit.

I tried to tear it out. I reached up and dug my fingers into the grille, trying to wrench it out, but I couldn't get hold of anything. The bugs are fixed too tight, and the grille is too strong to break. I picked at it, studied it, whacked it with the palm of my hand. I whacked it again. Punched it. Hard. But all that did was rip the skin off my knuckles.

And that's when I lost it.

Something inside me snapped, and I just started spitting and screaming at the grille like a lunatic. "You *BASTARD*! What do you *want*? Why don't you show your bastard face, eh? Why don't you *do* something? *WHAT DO YOU WANT?*"

He didn't answer me.

11:30 p.m.

I've calmed down a bit now. I've thought calm thoughts and silenced the rage in my head. Underneath it all, I'm still dead scared, and I'm still really angry, and I still feel like screaming my heart out, but I'm not on my own any more. I can't just do what *I* want to do. Ranting and raving about things might make me feel a little bit better, but it isn't going to do Jenny any good. She's got enough on her plate as it is. The last thing she needs is a madman for company.

She cried for a long time when she woke up this afternoon, big snotty tears that streamed down her face and soaked into her clothes. Then she curled up into a ball and lay on the floor for a while, muttering quietly to herself. I didn't like that, it worried me. I felt better when she started crying again. This time the sobbing wasn't quite so snotty and wet, but it was a lot wilder. She called out for her mum and dad, she shook and shivered, she wailed, she bawled.

I did my best.

I sat with her.

Watched over her.

She sobbed, she howled, her body heaved, and I just sat with her, crying a few silent tears myself.

I wish I could have done more to help her.

But I didn't have any more.

Later, after Jenny had cried herself dry, she said she was hungry. She didn't moan about it or anything. She just said, "I'm hungry."

"Me too," I told her.

"I bet you're not as hungry as me."

She was probably right. I don't actually feel that hungry any more. I know I am, though. A couple of times today I felt really tired, like I didn't have any energy left, and I'm sure it's because I haven't eaten anything for a long time. I'm not too worried about it yet. I've been hungry before. I know what it's like. You can go a long time without food.

Shit. Thinking about it has made me feel hungry again.

Anyway, it's a relief to know that Jenny's hungry. I mean, that's a good sign, isn't it? Like when you're ill and you don't have any appetite, and then you start getting better and you begin to feel hungry again.

That's good, isn't it?

I don't know.

What do I know? I'm just a kid. I'm sixteen years old. I don't know anything about looking after people. No one's ever looked after me, and I've only ever looked after myself.

But still, my gut feeling tells me that Jenny's feeling a bit better. It's not *good* that she's hungry, obviously. But I'd be a lot more worried if she wasn't.

Earlier on this evening, when I was putting the wheelchair back in the lift, Jenny asked me what the clear plastic thing on the wall was for. She called it a tray.

"What's that tray for, Linus?"

"I don't know."

She studied it for a while, then turned her attention to the one on the corridor wall. She looked thoughtful. Clear brown eyes, a curious little mouth.

"Why don't we ask him for some food?" she said. "Send him a note."

"He knows we're hungry," I said.

She reached up and took a sheet of paper from the leaflet-holder. "Maybe he wants us to ask. Some people are like that. They won't give you anything unless you ask."

I looked at her. She reached up and picked the pen off the wall, then crouched down, put the sheet of paper on the floor and got ready to write.

"What shall I ask for?" she said.

I couldn't help smiling. "Ask him to let us go."

She wrote: *Please let us go.*

"What else?" she said.

"Ask him what he wants."

She wrote: *What do you want.*

"Don't forget the question mark."

She added the question mark, then wrote: *Please give us some food. Bread. Cheese. Apples. Crisps. Choclate. Milk. And some tea.*

"You like tea?" I asked her.

"Uh-huh."

She wrote: *Soap. Towls. Toothbrushs and toothpaste.*

I said, "You're a good writer."

She gave me a look. "I'm not a *baby*."

"Sorry."

She nodded. "Anything else?"

"I think that should do it."

She wrote: *Thank you.* Then she stood up and placed the sheet of paper in the leaflet-holder in the lift and clipped the pen back on the wall.

"Do you think it'll work?" I asked her.

She shrugged, looking pleased with herself.

I said, "It doesn't really matter if it doesn't work, does it?"

"No."

"We won't be any worse off than we are now."

"Right."

I smiled. "I suppose you think you're pretty smart?"

"Smarter than you."

It's nearly midnight now. I've warned Jenny about the lights.

"They go off at twelve," I told her. "It gets very dark. But don't worry, they'll come on again in the morning."

"I'm not afraid of the dark," she said. "I like it."

She's sleeping in the bed in my room. I'm going to sleep on the floor. I got some blankets and pillows from the other beds and I've made myself a cosy little nest by the door. It reminds me a bit of the street. Blankets, cardboard, doorways.

Home from home.

I'm glad Jenny's not afraid of the dark.

I wish I wasn't.

Wednesday, 1 February

It's funny how things turn out. Five months ago I ran away to London to escape from the shittiness of school and the emotional madness of being at home. It wasn't easy, and I'm still not sure it was the right thing to do, but I did it. I fought and struggled to find what I was looking for, and although I never found it, I finally got used to the freedom of the streets and was beginning to get myself sorted out. And now here I am, stuck in the shittiest place in the world with my emotions being ripped to shreds.

Funny?

It's absolutely hilarious.

Maybe it's my ka*r*ama, as Lugless would say. "Tis your furkin' ka*r*ama, Linus boy. Yep yep. Indeedy-doo." Lugless. Good old Lug. The one-eared fool. I wonder what he's doing right now. Shuffling along the subway in his dirty old coat, probably. Muttering home-made mantras to himself and guzzling tap water from a cider bottle. Lugless always drinks water from a cider bottle, gallons of the stuff. I asked him once why he did it.

"Say what?" he said.

"Why do you drink water from a cider bottle? You know it winds up the winos."

"Wind 'em up. Yep. Yep."

"Is that why you do it?"

"Do what? Furkin' diddee."

"Never mind."

"Say what?"

Incoherent happiness.

Freedom.

Karma.

I'll have to think about that.

Jenny was already awake when the lights came on this morning. I dragged my head out from under the sheet, looked across the room, and there she was, sitting up in bed staring at me.

"You were dreaming," she said.

"Was I?"

"Our dog dreams. His legs twitch, and he whines."

"Is that what I was doing?"

"I think you were crying."

Great.

"What's he called?" I said. "Your dog."

"Woody."

"Good name."

"It's short for Woodbine."

She was fully dressed and still wearing my hooded jacket. The hood was up, almost covering her face. She looked like a miniature monk.

"Can I have a bath?" she asked.

"No."

"Why not?"

"There's no hot water."

"I don't mind. I'll have a cold bath."

I haven't told her about the cameras and the microphones yet. I don't want to frighten her. I'm frightened enough for both of us. And the thought of him sitting up there watching her in the bathroom, stealing her privacy... God, it makes me feel so sick.

"Let me check first," I said to her, getting up. "I'll see if there's any water. You stay here. I won't be a minute."

I went into the kitchen and turned on the cooker. While the ring was heating up, I ripped a patch of lining from my padded shirt and then fished the broken plastic fork from my pocket. When the ring was glowing red, I held the fork to the element, got it melting, then smeared dabs of molten plastic on the corners of the cloth square. Before they had a chance to cool down, I ran along the corridor, grabbed a chair from one of the rooms, then went into the bathroom. I positioned the chair under the grille, stood on it, then reached up and started to stick the cloth over the camera. The molten plastic was nearly dry now, and it didn't seem to be sticking too well to the cloth, but I reckoned if I pressed hard enough it might just work.

I never got the chance.

Just as I was moving the cloth into position the lights went out, plunging the bathroom into darkness, and a moment later something hot and pungent squirted out from the grille and set fire to my eyes. I don't know what it was. Gas, liquid... like an aerosol spray. Hot and hissy. It stung like hell. I screamed, dropped the cloth, put my hands to my eyes and fell off the chair.

I must have hit my head on something, the bath or the sink. I can't remember.

I blacked out for a while.

When I came round the lights were on again and Jenny was leaning over me, dabbing at my eyes with the dampened sleeve of my jacket.

"What happened?" she said. "Are you all right? Your eyes look funny."

"Funny?"

"They're all red and puffy."

I reached up and felt my head. There was an egg-sized lump just behind my ear. When I touched it, a red-hot knife speared through my skull.

"Does it hurt?" Jenny asked.

"Just a bit."

After that I had to tell her about the microphones and cameras. I didn't want to, and I didn't like doing it, but I couldn't see what else to do. What else *could* I do? I probably could have stopped her having a bath for a while, I probably could have thought up some excuse, but she'd still be washing, using the toilet, thinking she was alone when she wasn't. I can't watch her *all* the time. I mean, I'll work out something to put the cameras out of action, I'm not letting the bastard get away with it. But it's going to take time. And meanwhile we've got our bodily functions to consider.

I don't know what to do.

This place is driving me crazy.

When I told Jenny about the cameras she didn't say anything for a while, she just looked up at the grille, then back at me, then up at the grille again.

"He's watching us from up there?"

"I think so."

"All the time?"

28

I nodded. "Probably."

"What about...?" Her voice was close to tears. "What about in here? When I'm...you know?"

"It won't be for long," I said gently. "I'll think of something, I promise."

She was quiet for a long time. Staring at the floor, fiddling with the sleeve of my jacket, silent tears rolling down her cheeks. Eventually she looked up at me and said, "He's a bad man, isn't he?"

"Yeah, he's bad."

She nodded slowly and looked up at the ceiling. "You're a bad man, Mister. A very bad man."

12:30 p.m.

Well, what do you know? Jenny's idea worked. The food idea, the note. It actually worked. When the lift came down at nine o'clock, there was a shopping bag on the floor, and when we opened it up we found almost everything we'd asked him for: a loaf of sliced white bread, a packet of cheese, two apples, two Mars bars, two packets of crisps, a bottle of milk, a packet of tea bags, a bar of soap, two towels, two toothbrushes, and a tube of toothpaste.

"He didn't answer your question," Jenny said. "He didn't tell us what he wants."

"Who cares?" I said, smiling at her. "Let's eat."

We lugged the stuff out of the lift, put the towels and things in the bathroom, then got stuck into the food. Cheese sandwiches and crisps and Mars bars. I've never tasted anything so good in my life.

"Don't you want your apple?" Jenny asked.

29

"I'm allergic to fruit," I told her. "You can have it."

"Thanks." She took a huge bite and started chewing. "What happens if you eat fruit? Do you get a rash or something?"

"My head swells up."

She raised her eyebrows.

"Honestly," I said. "My head swells up, my eyes start bulging, and the skin starts peeling off my face."

She grinned. "You're making it up."

I reached for the apple. "Give me that and I'll show you."

She laughed and snatched it away. "No! I don't want to see you with a swelled-up head."

I puffed my cheeks and pulled a face.

She burped.

I laughed.

Just for now, things are all right.

We don't have a kettle or saucepans, and we don't have a hot tap, so we're having to make tea with cold water. It's not brilliant, but it's better than nothing.

We've just finished writing another note.

Kettle.
Saucepans.
Torch/candles.
Bread.
Butter.
Cheese.
Ham.
Milk.

Orange juice.
Cornflakes.
Bananas.
Chocolate.
Soup.
Crisps.
Chicken.
Fish fingers.
Carrots.
Beans.
Spaghetti Hoops.
Radio.
Television.
Mobile phone.

I added the last three items just for the hell of it.

Jenny insisted on writing *Thank you* at the bottom of the note.

When she wasn't looking, I added my own postscript: *Whatever it takes, Mister, whatever it takes.*

Later.

Today seems to have passed really quickly. The hours have just floated by. I suppose it's being with Jenny that does it. I'm used to being on my own, and I like it. I like being alone. I'm happy with myself. I've always thought that if I got marooned on a desert island or stuck in solitary confinement or something, I'd be OK. I'd manage. I could cope on my own. And I did, didn't I? I spent a while down here on my own. I didn't like it, but that wasn't because I was alone. Alone had nothing to do with it. I didn't like it because there's nothing to like down here, simple as that. So, yeah, I can cope on my own. But I have to admit it's pretty good to have someone else around. Someone to talk to, someone to react with. It makes me feel better.

It doesn't make things any less crap, of course. Or less scary. Or less anything, really. But it's all right.

It's just gone 9 p.m. now. The lift has gone up.

Jenny's reading the bible.

I'm sitting in my nest, talking to you, to me, to you . . .

Now there's a thought. Who *are* you?

Who *am* I talking to?

I don't know.

I have no one in mind for *you*. I know you're somewhere, but right now you're nowhere, and I'm talking to myself.

I have to think about the cameras.

Midnight, lights out.

Thursday, 2 February

This morning the lift came down with most of the stuff we'd asked for. No torch or candles (and obviously no radio, TV, or mobile phone), but we got the kettle, an aluminium saucepan—both brand new—and all the food and drink we'd asked for, except the chicken. I don't know what that means. Nothing, probably. There was also a new plastic fork to replace the one I chopped up and melted.

The kettle is one of those old-fashioned whistling things that you boil up on the cooker. There aren't any electric sockets in here. The cooker and the fridge are bolted to the floor, so I can't tell how they're connected. I expect the cables are threaded through the wall. I'll have to look into that. There's a lot of things I need to look into. Like how to get out of here, how to sort out the cameras, how to keep things from getting too manky.

The smell, for instance.

Things are starting to stink a bit. We've both been washing fairly regularly, but it doesn't matter how often you wash if you wear the same clothes all the time. You can't help smelling bad. And anyway, with the cameras watching us, it's not easy to feel good about stripping off to have a good wash. The rest of it is bad enough. Jenny won't go to the toilet unless the lights are out. I don't know how she manages. I just try to ignore the cameras. Ignore him. Pretend he's not there. No cameras, no one watching. Close your eyes, imagine you're somewhere else, believe it.

Believe it, that's the thing. Believe your own lies.

The smell of unwashed bodies isn't very nice, but I don't mind it too much. I'm used to it. I always kept myself pretty clean on the streets, but a lot of them don't bother. I don't think Lugless *ever* washed. It's understandable. So you smell a bit, so what? Everyone smells. It's no big deal. And once your body odour reaches a certain level it doesn't really get any worse anyway. So why bother trying to keep clean? What do you get out of it? Not much. I only made the effort because, for some reason, when I look dirty I look *really* dirty. Nasty-dirty, like something that's crawled out from under a rock. My hair is quite long, and if I don't give it a brush now and then, or at least run my fingers through it, it mats up into ratty old ropes and makes me look like a mad person. And if I don't wash, my skin gets kind of greyish, which gives me the sickly look of a junkie. I don't particularly mind looking like a mad junkie, but it doesn't help when I'm busking. People don't mind giving money to a sweet-looking homeless kid, but when they see a wild-haired loony on the street they tend to assume he's going to blow the cash on crack or heroin or something, and to them that's *bad*. That's *wrong*. W-R-O-N-G. It's bad enough begging for fags and booze, but drugs? Oh, no. I'm not giving *my* money to a drug addict.

Take Windsor Jack, for example. Windsor's not that handsome, kind of beaky-nosed and mean-looking, and he's only got one leg. Well, one and a half legs, actually. He fell asleep one night when he was mashed out of his head, slept for twenty-eight hours with his leg all twisted up under his body, and when he woke up it was dead, useless, no blood. Lost it from the knee down. Anyway, Windsor just sits on the street all day holding out his hand. He doesn't say anything, no cardboard sign, nothing. Just sits there showing off his stump and holding out his hand, hoping for sympathy cash. But he never gets much because he looks so mean and ugly, and he's *always* off his head. Staring eyes, blank face, zombified. He might as well have DRUG ADDICT tattooed on his forehead. Someone gave him a sandwich once. A sniffy old lady in a beige raincoat. I was busking nearby and I saw her lean down and place a pre-packed sandwich in his hand. She told him to lay off the drugs and get some food inside him. Windsor stared at the sandwich like it was a dog turd. Then, as the old lady walked off, he looked up and chucked it at the back of her head.

Later.

Things have changed. They changed at noon. Jenny was in the kitchen eating a bowl of cornflakes, and I was sitting at the table staring at the grille on the ceiling, trying to work out how to kill the cameras without getting a face full of poison. Everything was quiet. Everything was normal. Everything was routine. There's always a routine, wherever you are. You soon get used to it. Lights on at eight, lift down at nine. Lift up again at nine in the evening, lights off at twelve. Long hours of doing nothing. Waiting, thinking, sitting around, lying down, standing up, walking in circles. I don't like it, but I'm getting used to it, and once you're used to something it never feels quite so bad.

So there I was, sitting at the table, staring at the ceiling, deep in thought, thinking of plots and plans, hats, masks, shields, covers, when all at once the lift door closed—*tkk-kshhh-mmm*—and the lift whirred into action.

Nnnnnnn . . .

I looked at the clock.

Twelve o'clock?

The lift doesn't go up at twelve o'clock.

Not routine.

Not good.

Jenny came out of the kitchen wiping milk from her chin. "What's that noise?"

"The lift."

She glanced instinctively at the clock. "What's happening?"

"I don't know."

I got up from the table, went over to the lift door, and listened. The humming had stopped. The lift had reached the top.

I turned to Jenny. "Get back in the kitchen."

"Why?"

"Just do it, please."

"Why? What's happening?"

"I don't know. Please, just get back in the kitchen."

From above I heard the sound of the lift starting up again—*g-dung, g-dunk, clunk, click, nnnnnnnn . . .*

Jenny's eyes grew frightened.

"Don't worry," I told her. "It's probably nothing. Just wait in the kitchen while I see what's happening. Shut the door, OK? I'll call you out in a minute."

She hesitated, staring at the lift door.

"Go on," I said.

She backed into the kitchen and shut the door. I turned to

face the lift. It whirred down and *g-dunk*ed to a halt. My heart was beating hard now and my hands were sweating. I wiped them on my shirt and took a deep breath. The lift door opened—*mmm-kshhh-tkk . . .*

There were two people inside. A woman in the wheelchair and a man slumped on the floor with his feet bound and his hands tied behind his back. The woman was unconscious. She'd been drugged, just like me and Jenny. I could smell the stuff on her breath—bitter, sweet, horrible. Her make-up was all smudged and a dribble of sick had dried on her mouth. The man was awake, but he didn't look too good. His mouth was tied with a bloodstained gag, his nose was bleeding, and his left eye was swollen shut. The right eye stared furiously at me.

"*Unh!*" he muttered through the gag. "*Furngehissoh! Nunhh!*"

I was pretty shocked, but nowhere near as stunned as I'd been when Jenny arrived. I'm not sure why. They were adults, I suppose. It's different with adults, isn't it? When you see an adult in trouble you still feel bad, but not half as bad as when you see a child in trouble. It's the helplessness, I suppose. It gets to you. Whacks you in the heart. Or maybe not. Maybe it's just me. Maybe I've just got something against adults.

Whatever.

I wasn't paralysed this time.

I wheeled the woman out first, then called Jenny and went back for the man. He was big, too heavy to drag, so I started on the ropes round his wrists. They were knotted tight.

Jenny came over and cautiously approached the woman.

"Get some water," I told her.

"Who is she?" she said, looking at the woman. Then she looked at the man. "And who's *that*?"

"I don't know yet. Get some water, please."

She went back into the kitchen, and I carried on struggling with the ropes. The man was kicking his feet.

"*Nunh uhh uhh . . .* "

"Keep still," I told him.

"*Norighfurnge . . . nunh . . .* "

"Keep *still*, for Christ's sake."

After a couple of minutes I finally got the knots untied. The man whipped his arms free and yanked the gag from his mouth.

"*Fuck!*" he spluttered, shaking some life into his hands. "Why didn't you take the fucking *gag* off first? Shit! I couldn't fucking *breathe*, man!"

He's big. A *very* big man. Tall. Solid. Hard as nails. Greasy hands, short dusty hair. Work jeans, boots, a faded sweatshirt with the sleeves cut off.

He sat up and started to untie his feet, tugging at the ropes and looking around with his one good eye.

"What is this shit?" he said. "Who are you? Where's the fucking wanker—?"

"Hey," I said.

He stopped talking and glared at me.

"I'm on your side," I told him. "I'm trying to help. Why don't you just shut up a minute and let me deal with the lady. All right?"

He gave me a hard look. *Very* hard. He sniffed a dribble of blood up his nose and wiped his mouth with the back of his hand. Then he looked over at the woman in the wheelchair. She was beginning to come round now, groaning and mumbling and holding her head. Jenny was standing beside her with a cup of water in her hand, staring wide-eyed at me and the big man. Scared to death.

The big man said, "Shit," and went back to untying his feet.

I went over to the woman. Jenny was helping her to drink some water, holding the cup to her lips. As I approached, the woman pushed the cup away, lurched forward in the wheelchair, and threw up on the floor.

The big man's called Fred.

"Fred what?" I asked him.

"Just Fred."

Right.

The woman's name is Anja. Pronounced *Anya*, like Tanya without the T. Anja Mason. She's one of those confident women who always get what they want. Late twenties, well-spoken, honey-blonde hair, a fine nose, sculpted mouth, perfect teeth, silver necklace round her neck. Dressed in a sheer white top, short black skirt, tights, and high heels.

My dad would love her.

She says she's "in property," whatever that means. Selling houses, I suppose. That's how he got her. She'd made an appointment to show a Mr. Fowles around a luxury ground-floor flat in a secluded avenue in West London. Ten o'clock this morning. She turned up alone. Parked her car. Mr. Fowles was waiting for her on the front step. He smiled, said good morning. She opened the door and showed him in. He seemed pleasant enough.

"Did he say anything else to you?" I asked her.

She thought about it. "No, not really. Not that I can recall."

"Nothing?"

A hint of annoyance crept into her voice. "I can't *remember*, OK?"

She showed him the hallway, she told us, showed him the living room, then took him into the kitchen. While she was pointing out the parquet flooring, he got her with the chloroform. She says she knows it was chloroform because her husband works "in chemicals."

At this, Fred laughed. "You *what*?"

"What?" said Anja.

"*How* do you know it was chloroform?"

"My husband," she repeated. "He's a company manager with a multinational chemical company."

"What, in the fucking *chloroform* department?"

She gave him an icy look. "What's your problem?"

Fred didn't answer, just grinned hard and scratched his arm.

I know what his problem is. He's a junkie, a heroin addict. I can tell from the way he walks, the look in his eyes, the way he holds himself. The track marks on his arms.

"How long has it been?" I asked him.

He sniffed and jerked his head. "What?"

I mimed injecting a needle.

He shrugged and rubbed his arm again. "This morning, couple of hours before the van hit me."

He says he does body work at a shop in Camden Town, and I'm sure he does, but I don't think that's the whole story. I know a thief when I see one. Thief, dealer, hard man, crook. You name it, he'll probably do it. He's that kind of man. Last night, he says, he was out and about somewhere in Essex. Doesn't remember where, he says. Got lost, he says. Someone stole his car.

Yeah, right.

At eleven o'clock this morning he was still stuck in the middle of nowhere, trying to find his way back to London. Hitching, looking for a railway station, trying to find a car to steal. He was walking along a narrow country lane when he heard a van. He turned round to stick his thumb out, the van drove into him, caught him a glancing blow and knocked him into a ditch.

"Hurt like fuck," he said, rubbing his shoulder. "I thought it was broke. And then, when I start crawling out of the ditch, all covered in leaves and mud and shit, someone whacks me across the head with an iron bar." As an afterthought, he smiled at Anja and said, "I know it was an iron bar because *my wife* works in an iron-bar factory."

Anja pouted. "Very funny."

It *was* pretty funny.

Fred went on. "That was it. Out cold. I think he gave me another couple of whacks just to make sure, then he must have got me in the van and tied me up. Next thing I know I'm being bundled into a fucking lift." He shook his head. "He's a strong bastard, I'll give him that."

He rubbed his arm again and wiped sweat from his brow.

"Are you all right?" I asked him.

"Starting to feel it."

"Bad?"

"It will be."

"Do you want anything?"

"What have you got?"

"Not much. Tea, water..."

"*Tea?*"

41

I shrugged.

"Any aspirin?"

"I've asked for some."

It was gone ten o'clock now, so the lift had already gone up for the night. I'd put in a fresh shopping list. Food, aspirin, bandages, juice, cigarettes for Anja and Fred.

It was at this point that Anja suddenly recognized Jenny. "Oh, *God*!" she gasped, staring at her. "You're *her*, aren't you? You're that girl from the news, the one that went missing? Oh, shit . . . what *is* this? What the *hell's* going on here?"

I told her and Fred as much as I know, which isn't much. I told them how Jenny and me were captured. I told them about the lift, and how we have to ask for things. And I told them about the lights, the cameras, the microphones.

When Anja realized what the cameras meant, she almost had a fit.

"He's *what*?"

"Watching us," I said. "Listening."

"Why?"

"I don't know."

She stared at me. "Are you seriously telling me that everywhere I go this dirty old man is *watching* me?"

"That's right."

"*Everywhere?*"

"Yes," I sighed.

"Oh, my *God*! That's dis*gus*ting. I'm not having that. You have to do something. You have to get me out of here."

"Me?" I said.

"I don't care *who*," she whined. "I just want to get out of here. *Now*." She rolled her eyes. "This is im*poss*ible. I have

42

commitments... I have things to *do*." She started crying. "I have to get *out* of here."

I turned to Fred.

"So," he sniffed. "No aspirin till tomorrow?"

"Nine o'clock in the morning, if he agrees."

"No cigarettes till then either?"

"Nope."

"Shit."

Later again.

Now that Fred and Anja are here, everything feels different, and I'm not sure I like it. I know there was nothing to like about anything before they were here, but I suppose I'd kind of got used to things as they were—just me and Jenny, doing our best to look after each other.

But now...?

I don't know.

I feel sort of edgy, unsettled.

Out of place.

I just don't like it.

I'm tired.

It's been a long day.

I'll write some more tomorrow.

Friday, 3 February

Last night it occurred to me that Jenny might feel more comfortable sleeping in Anja's room rather than sharing with me. But when I mentioned it to her, she got all snotty about it.

"I thought you liked me?"

"I do."

"I thought we were friends?"

"We are. It's just . . ."

"Just what?"

"Well, you're a girl."

"So?"

"And I'm a boy."

"So?"

I sighed. "All I meant was—"

"I don't *like* Anja."

"Why not?"

"She's scary. She sticks her nose up."

"That's just her way. It doesn't mean anything."

"I don't like her."

"I'm sure she's all right."

"Why don't *you* sleep in her room then?"

"Very funny."

Jenny grinned.

And that was that.

There were no more surprises when the lift came down this morning, just a shopping bag full of food. No aspirins, no bandages, no cigarettes. Me and Jenny put the food away and started making breakfast, then Anja came in. No make-up, bleary eyes, crumpled clothes. She looked tired and fragile, and somehow that made her seem more approachable.

Or so I thought.

"Morning," I said.

"What?"

"Good morning."

She just glared at me. "Any cigarettes?"

"I'm afraid not."

"Shit!" she hissed. "*Shit!*"

She turned round and stomped out.

I looked at Jenny.

Jenny shrugged.

We got on with breakfast, eating silently, like a couple of kids whose mum is in a really bad mood. When Anja stomped back in again to get a drink of water, muttering more curses under her breath, I sneaked a glance across the table at Jenny and saw her looking back at me with a smug glint in her eye, as if to say, "See? What did I tell you? She's *scary*."

Just so you know, this is where everyone is:

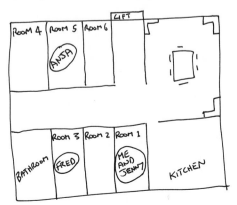

Notice anything odd about that?

Maybe it's just a coincidence, but apart from me and Jenny it seems like we're all trying to keep as far away from each other as possible. Which is kind of strange, don't you think? I mean, here we all are, stuck together in this hellish situation, desperate to find a way out, and we're behaving like strangers on a bus.

Or maybe it's not so strange after all?

It's just what people do, I suppose.

After breakfast I went to see how Fred was doing. There was no answer when I knocked on his door. I knocked again and put my ear to the door. Nothing. I called out his name, knocked again, then opened the door and looked in. He was lying on the bed, curled up into a ball, wearing nothing but a pair of shorts. The bedclothes were all thrown on the floor, and I could see scars and tattoos all over his body, needle tracks on his arms and legs. He's got a lot of scars. He had the pillow clamped over his head and he was sweating like mad and moaning like a baby.

Heroin withdrawal.

Even with his legs all scrunched up, the bed's far too small for him. He must be at least six feet four.

"How's it going?" I asked him.

"*Unnnhh*," he replied.

"Do you want some tea?"

"*Unh*."

"We didn't get any aspirins. You'll have to stick it out."

"*Funnhh* . . . "

"I'll bring you some tea."

On the way back to the kitchen, I passed Anja's room. The

door was open and I could see her sitting on the bed with her legs crossed and her arms held tightly across her chest.

Jenny's right about her, she is scary. Beautiful but scary. She has that overbearing confidence that comes from wealth and good looks.

"Do you want something to eat?" I asked her.

Her head snapped round at the sound of my voice. "What?"

"Would you like anything to eat?"

"How long are we going to be here?"

"I've no idea."

She flicked at her hair. "It's un*bear*able." She started jiggling her foot up and down, then turned and looked at me. A good long look, up and down, checking me out like I was piece of furniture or something. Finally she blinked, wrinkled her nose, and looked away.

"What are the police doing about Jenny?" I asked her.

"What?"

I sighed. "What are they saying on the news about Jenny?"

"Jenny who?"

I glared at her.

"Oh, right," she said. "The girl . . ." She shrugged. "I think there was one of those appeals on TV, you know, a press conference, with her parents and everything. And there's been lots of coverage about her in the newspapers, lots of photographs, that kind of thing."

"Do the police have any leads?"

Anja shrugged again. "How should I know?"

"Did they *say* they had any leads?"

"I haven't really been following the story, to be honest. I'm very busy at the moment. I don't have time to—"

"You need to get your head out of your arse," I said.

"Ex*cuse* me?"

"You heard me. Stop feeling sorry for yourself, for Christ's sake."

She gave me a nasty look.

"You could try talking to Jenny for a start," I went on. "I know it's hard, but pretend you've got a heart."

She shook her head. "I don't have to listen to this."

I shrugged.

"What do *you* know anyway?" she sneered. "How old are you?"

"Old enough."

That was supposed to sound cool, but it probably didn't.

Her foot was jiggling around at sixty miles an hour.

I said, "You should have gone while it was dark."

"I'm *sorry*?"

"The toilet. I told you last night. You should have gone while it was dark."

She uncrossed her legs, brushed at her knee, flicked at something on her shoe, then recrossed her legs.

I said, "Do you want me to go with you?"

"What? God, no!"

"I won't look. I'll stand in front of you, facing away, so the camera won't see anything."

Her mouth tightened. She chewed her lip, stared hard at me, then looked away. The room was quiet.

I gave it a minute, then turned to leave.

At the door I heard a little sob. I turned round. Anja's head was bowed down and her voice was trembling. "Why's he *doing* this?" she wept. "What have *I* done? I don't deserve this. It's not *fair*."

"Fair doesn't come into it."

Tears rolled down her cheeks.

I said, "I'll be in the kitchen if you need me."

The summer before I ran away was a hot one. Long, hot, and tedious. Dad wasn't home very much, as usual, and I spent most of the school holidays either traipsing around the world with him, staying in hotels and soulless apartments, or—when he got fed up with me cramping his style—staying with various friends and relatives, most of whom I neither knew nor liked. I didn't actually get to spend any time at home with Dad until the week before I was due back at school. And even then, all we did was argue about stuff all the time. Mostly the same old stuff.

"I don't see *why* I have to go to boarding school, Dad. Why can't I just go to a normal school, a *local* school?"

"You know why, Linus. We've already been through this a million times."

"Yeah, but—"

"Just give it another year, OK? Once I've got all these projects sorted out I won't have to keep travelling so much, and then—"

"You said that last year."

"I know. But—"

"*And* the year before."

"Things are different now. I promise. This time next year everything will be OK."

That's when I decided it was time to go.

11:55 p.m.

I only wrote a short shopping list tonight. We've got enough food for tomorrow, so all I asked for was some clean clothes and something to read. I didn't bother asking the others if they wanted anything. I'm getting a bit sick of being mother. They know how it works. If they want something they can ask for it themselves.

After I'd put the note in the lift I stayed in there for a while, staring up at the camera. I knew it was pointless, but I did it anyway. I was feeling all gripey and irritable, and I couldn't think of anything else to do. So I just stood there, staring up at the camera, waiting to see what happened. Nine o'clock came and went and the lift didn't move.

"Go on," I said to the ceiling. "Beam me up. I promise I won't do anything. I just want to see you, have a little chat."

Nothing happened.

I smiled. "What's the matter? Don't you trust me?"

Nothing.

I waited another minute, then sighed and stepped out. As soon as I cleared the door, the lift started to hum, and I immediately jumped back in again.

It stopped humming.

I looked at the ceiling. "I suppose if I push this too far you're going do something unpleasant, aren't you?"

The silence was beginning to annoy me.

"All right," I said, stepping out. "I'll catch you later."

As I walked down the corridor I heard the lift start up. The door closed, the hum hummed, and the lift went up. I went to the bathroom, ran a cold bath, and got in fully dressed.

Now it's nearly lights-out time. My clothes are still soaking wet and I'm lying under a blanket, shivering. I think he's turned the heating down. Vindictive bastard.

But at least I'm clean.

Jenny's been quiet all night.

Anja hasn't shown her face since this morning.

Fred's making the occasional howling noise.

I've had an idea about the camera in the bathroom.

Saturday, 4 February

No new clothes, nothing to read. Fred's still out of action. I've solved the bathroom problem and been electrocuted.

When the lights came on this morning I showed Jenny my bathroom idea. It's so simple I feel like an idiot for not thinking of it before. Jenny tried it out first. When she came back she was grinning all over.

"How was it?" I asked.

"Brilliant."

Her face was radiant. It was wonderful to see. I wanted to stay there soaking it up, just bathing in her joy, but it made me feel *too* good. It was almost embarrassing.

"Well," I said, "I suppose I'd better go and give Miss Snooty the news."

I went along to Anja's room, knocked, waited for her to answer, then went in. She was still in bed. The room smelled bad. Her eyes were all puffy and her hair was knotted and dull.

"Yes?" she said.

There was a packet of cornflakes on the floor and a big chunk of bread on her bedside cabinet.

"Yes?" she repeated.

"How are you today?"

"What do you want?"

I glanced at the bread. "Midnight snack?"

"I was hungry."

"You *can* eat with us, you know. We're not savages."

"Did you want something?"

I held up the sheet I was carrying in my hand. "Privacy."

"What?"

I showed her the head-sized hole I'd torn in the sheet. "You just slip it on," I explained, "like a poncho. You can go to the bathroom, have a wash, use the toilet, and he can't see a thing."

"Is that it?"

I looked at her. "I thought you'd be pleased."

"Ecstatic, I'm sure."

I couldn't think of anything to say. I stared at her. She was lying quite awkwardly, kind of scrunched down low in the bed with her knees raised and one arm under the blanket. The other hand was fiddling nervously with the silver necklace round her neck.

I sniffed the air, looked round the room, then looked back at her.

"What?" she said.

"I'll be back in a minute."

I left her room and went down the corridor into the kitchen. I looked in the sink, then in the cupboard, then under the sink. I stood there for a moment, looking all round the kitchen, then I went back to Anja's room. She was sitting up straight with the sheet pulled up tight to her chest.

"Would you mind telling me what you're doing?" she snapped.

"Where is it?"

"Where's what?"

"The washing-up bowl you've been peeing in."

"The *what*?"

She was trying to sound disgusted and hurt, but it didn't quite work.

I sighed. "The washing-up bowl from the kitchen is missing. My bet is that you're hiding it under your sheet. You've been peeing in it, haven't you? I can smell it from here."

"How *dare* you?"

I suddenly felt very tired.

"Listen, lady," I said, "I know it's not nice being watched all the time, but we're all in this together. Think about what you're doing. You pee in the washing-up bowl, you empty it out in the bathroom, you put it back in the sink. We wash our plates in the bowl, we eat off the plates, we get germs from your piss, we get sick, we die. Is that what you want?"

Her face was bright red. "I was going to—"

"No, you weren't. Look, you can't just think about yourself all the time. You can't just hide away in here and hope that everything will go away."

Her eyes blazed for a second, then she looked down, ashamed. "I'm scared."

"We're all scared." I picked up the poncho/sheet and threw it on the bed. "If you need to use the toilet, use that. And make sure you wash the bowl thoroughly when you put it back."

God, this place is getting to me.

After the lift went up this evening I spent some time staring at the closed door. Staring and thinking. Thinking and staring. It's a hell of a door. Smooth, silver, grainy, solid, sealed. No gaps at the side, no gaps at the top, no gaps at the bottom. No markings. No flaws. No scratches.

After staring at it for a while I got a saucepan from the kitchen and gave the door a good hard whack. It didn't do any good, but it made me feel a bit better. I hit it a few more times, then kicked it, then dropped the pan and slapped the door with both hands. A bolt of lightning shot through my body and knocked me to the floor.

The door was electrified.

That was two hours ago.

My hands are still tingling.

Tomorrow is Sunday. I've been here a week. Seven days. Sometimes it feels like a lifetime, other times it feels like no time at all.

Memories come and go.

Home, the house we lived in before Mum died. Dad. School. The station, the subways, the big metal sculpture at Broadgate . . . it's all gone for now, another world, another planet. Light years away. But the little things . . . I still remember the little things. Half-formed memories of growing up, little stories, myths. Moments. Street things. Timeless things. And things that aren't so timeless. Like last Sunday morning. I can still remember the feel of the platform under my feet, the smooth grey concrete, cold and flat. I can feel the weight of my guitar digging into my shoulder. I can hear the *dong* of the E-string as the guitar bounces against my back. What else can I hear? Sunday morning sounds. Pigeons scuffling about. Early morning traffic. The big platform-guy's steel-tipped shoes clack-clacking on the concourse. Bully-boy shoes. Clack clack. Clack clack. Clack

clack. Then the sounds fade, the film in my head jumps forward, and I'm in the back of the blind man's van. The van lurches on its springs, and I know he's climbed up behind me, and I know I've been had, but it's already too late. He grabs my head and clamps a wet cloth over my face, and I start to choke. I'm breathing in chemicals. I can't breathe. There's no air. My lungs are on fire. I think I'm dying. I struggle, lashing out with my elbows and legs, kicking, stamping, jerking my head around like a madman, but it's no good. He's strong, a lot stronger than he looks. His hands grip my skull like a couple of vices. After a few seconds I start to feel dizzy, and then . . .

Nothing.

Next thing I know it's seven days later and I'm still sitting here thinking about it. And what's really annoying is I'm no wiser now than I was then. I still don't know where I am. I still don't know what I'm doing here. I still don't know what he wants. I still don't know how to get out. I still don't know what the future holds. I still don't know what I'm going to do.

I can't stand it.

I hate it. Even this, this stupid notebook, this diary, whatever it is. I despise it. I mean, what's the point of it anyway? Who am I writing *to*? Who are you? Why am I talking to you? What are you going to do to help me?

Nothing.

Less than nothing.

If you exist, if you're reading this, then I'm probably dead. Because if I ever get out of here the first thing I'm going to do is burn this notebook. Burn *you*. You won't exist any more. But then . . .

56

Just a minute.

If I get out of here and burn you, if I delete your existence, does that mean you won't *ever* have existed?

Shit, that's hard thinking.

Let me think.

You *have* to exist now. Otherwise I'm dead.

But I'm not. And neither of us knows how this is going to end . . .

So that means . . .

Shit.

I can't be bothered with it.

I don't feel well.

I'm going to sleep.

Sunday, 5 February

It's sometime in the afternoon. I've had really bad diarrhea all day. My mouth is dry and my belly hurts.

I can't get out of bed.

No energy to write.

Later, evening.

I'm still in bed. I don't know what time it is. I've been asleep. I can hear the others talking in the kitchen. Jenny, Anja, Fred. It's a comforting sound, but kind of depressing too. I feel left out. Everyone's finally talking to each other and I'm too sick to be there. It's not fair.

Fair doesn't come into it.

Later still.

My stomach seems to have settled down. It's still hurting a bit, but it's not too bad. Just a dull ache, deep down inside me. I haven't had to go to the bathroom for a while, which is good. Constant diarrhea is a really shitty thing to have. No joke. Diarrhea, bubbling guts, bad smells . . . *very* bad smells. This room absolutely *stinks*.

Jenny's been bringing me bowls of soup all evening. Hot soup, hot milk, cold towels. I keep telling her I don't want to eat anything, but she keeps on bringing it anyway. Just in case, she says. Every time she comes in she tries not to wrinkle her nose at the smell, but she can't help it. I don't blame her. It's a nose-wrinkling smell.

I've insisted she sleeps somewhere else tonight.

"But you need looking after," she said.

"Whatever I've got might be catching," I explained. "Who's going to look after me if you get ill?"

"Well . . ." She wrinkled her nose again. "I suppose I *could* sleep in the room next door."

"At least you'll be able to breathe."

She smiled awkwardly.

"Look," I said. "I'll leave my door open, OK? If I need you, I'll knock on the wall. And if you need me—"

"I'll whistle. I'm a good whistler."

She whistled, just to show me what she meant. Then she picked up the tray of cold soup and left.

Fred popped in a while ago. He says he still feels like shit, but he thinks he's over the worst of it now. He doesn't look too good. He's lost a lot of weight. His eyes are kind of watery and his nose is all runny. He looks like someone who's just getting over a really bad dose of flu. He didn't say much, just asked me how I was doing, hoped I was getting better, that kind of thing. It felt odd at first, being alone in a tiny little room with this grizzly-bear-sized man. It made me feel a bit edgy. A bit cramped. After a while though, after I'd realized he wasn't going to eat me or anything, I started to relax a bit. I talked to him. I asked him how he was doing, what he thought about things—escaping, getting out, that kind of thing. It was kind of OK, just the two of us, talking about stuff. Strangely relaxing. At one point he even smiled at me. He's got surprisingly nice teeth. Smaller than I imagined. Whiter too.

I don't know what kind of teeth I expected him to have. Maybe tattooed ones, or fangs or something.

Before he left he gave me a friendly pat on the arm. You know, one of those man-to-man/see-you-later-mate pats. I don't think anyone's ever done that to me before.

It felt pretty good.

I'm beginning to like him.

About ten minutes after Fred left, Anja came in. She brought me a cup of tea. First thing she said was, "I can't stay long." Like she'd got somewhere really important to rush off to. I nodded at her. She just stood there holding the cup of tea. I think she wanted to thank me for not telling the others about our little secret. You know, the peeing-in-the-bowl thing. I could see it in her eyes. Uncertainty, guilt, conflict. She *wanted* to thank me, but when the moment actually came, she chickened out. Her breeding got the better of her. She smiled a tight smile, put the tea on the cabinet, and scuttled out.

I sighed to myself and reached for the cup.

The tea was disgusting.

Monday, 6 February

Now we're five.

When the lights came on this morning the lift was already down and a fat man in a grey suit was asleep on the floor. Fred found him. He's got his appetite back now and he was up early looking for something to eat. He heard a snoring sound coming from the lift. He saw the fat man, dragged him out, then yelled for us to come and see.

We went and saw.

Jenny first, then Anja, then me.

I don't know if it was just because I'd spent the last day in bed, but the image of the three of us stumbling out of our rooms and crossing to the lift really got me down. Our appearance—bedraggled and pale, heavy-footed, weary-eyed—and the way we walked, with the passionless excitement of death-row prisoners . . .

God, we all looked so weak, so hopeless.

Fred was standing proudly over the fat man, like a cat with a dead mouse.

"Hey," he said. "Look what I got."

We looked. The man was in his late thirties, fat, with curly black hair and dandruff on the collar of his suit. He was lying on his side, snoring loudly, with the tip of his tongue poking out from between his lips.

I bent down to check his pulse.

"He stinks of booze," I said.

Fred sniffed. "Drugged?"

"Maybe. I can't smell any chloroform though."

I leaned closer. The fat man opened his eyes, coughed once, then puked.

His name is William Bird. He's a commuter. Lives in a village near Chelmsford, works in London, in the City. Management consultant or something. Yesterday evening, after work, he met a man in a bar at Liverpool Street station. An unremarkable-looking man, he said. Suit, raincoat, glasses, moustache. This man was also going to Chelmsford. They shared a few drinks, talked about money and cars, then got on the train together and shared a few more drinks from the trolley.

"I remember getting on the train," Bird said. "But after that . . ." He shook his head. "It's all just a blur. I must have passed out."

"Pissed?" asked Fred.

"Not *that* much."

Fred looked at me. "Roofies, probably. Or Special K. Something like that."

I nodded. Roofies is the street-name for Rohypnol, a drug that knocks you out and makes you forget everything. Stick a couple of roofies in someone's drink and they won't know *what's* going on. Special K is ketamine hydrochloride, an animal tranquillizer.

Bird looked at me. "Don't I know you from somewhere?"

Yeah, I thought. You've probably walked past me at Liverpool Street about a hundred times. You've probably given me a hundred dirty looks, or ignored me, or chucked your empty fag packet in my guitar case.

"I don't think so," I said.

Bird loosened his tie and looked around. "What the hell *is* this place anyway? What's going on? I've got a meeting at three."

I left the others to give him the good news and went back to my room for a lie-down. I wasn't feeling too bad, but I still didn't feel up to much. I certainly didn't feel up to explaining to a fat commuter that he was imprisoned in some kind of underground bunker by an unknown man with unknown intentions, that there was no way out, nothing to do, no privacy, no life, no hope, no *NOTHING*. That we could all be here for years...

We could be here for years.

No, I didn't feel up to that.

I'm going to sleep.

Woken by the sound of shouts and crashing metal, then the lights went out and a high-pitched whistle screamed through my head. The loudest, most agonizing sound I've ever heard. It probably only lasted about thirty seconds or so, but it felt like eternity. I thought my skull was going to crack.

I still had my hands clamped over my ears when the lights came on again and Jenny rushed in and told me what had happened. Apparently, Fred attacked one of the cameras with a saucepan. To protect himself from getting sprayed, he'd covered his head with a sheet and wrapped his hands with bits of torn T-shirt.

"What happened to him?" I asked Jenny. My ears were still ringing and my voice sounded muffled.

Jenny waggled her hand. "He got a couple of good hits in,

then the spray came on and soaked through the sheet and he started yelling."

"Any damage?"

"What?"

"Any *damage*?"

"Not to the camera."

"How about Fred?"

"His eyes and his face got burned and he hurt his arm when he fell off the chair. His ears are bleeding too."

"From the whistle?"

She dug a finger in her ear. "What?"

"The *whistle*."

"It hurt my ears."

"I know."

There didn't seem much else to say. Jenny looked at me. I shrugged. She gave her ears another dig, then winced.

"Why's he doing this to us, Linus?" she said, wiping a tear from her eye. "Why's he so bad?"

"I don't know. Some people are just like that, I suppose. They like being bad."

"Why?"

"I don't know."

A couple of months ago I got beaten up by a bunch of stockbrokers. I think they were stockbrokers anyway. Stockbrokers, bankers, traders, something like that. There were six or seven of them. Young men in sharp suits and expensive haircuts. It was a Friday night, about eight o'clock. Cold and drizzly. Damp. I was busking around Princes Street. There are loads of wine bars around there and they always get really busy on a Friday evening. You know, end of the day, end of the week, start of the weekend, let's all go out and have a good time—that kind of thing. Anyway, I thought I might get lucky, tug a few drunken heartstrings, get some cash. So I found myself a nice little sheltered spot in the doorway of an office building, got my guitar out, laid the case on the ground, and started to play. And I was doing pretty well too. A nice pile of 50ps, pound coins, a few two-pounders. I'd even got a screwed-up fiver from someone.

Then they showed up—the stockbrokers, the men in sharp suits. They were all good and drunk and working hard to enjoy themselves. Loud-mouthed, red-faced, laughing and pushing each other around. As they walked past me one of them tripped over the kerb and stumbled into the doorway, crashing into my guitar case and knocking it over. The coins tumbled out and rolled all over the place—along the pavement, under people's feet, into the rain-soaked gutter. I stopped playing and looked down at the drunken idiot crawling around on his knees at my feet. He had gelled hair and neat little sideburns and he was laughing like an idiot and grabbing at the coins, throwing them at his mates.

"You stupid shit," I said to him.

He stopped laughing and glared at me. "You what?"

"That's my money you're chucking away."

"Yeah?"

"Yeah."

He picked up a pound coin. "You call this money?"

I was beginning to wish I hadn't said anything now. His friends had shuffled over and were standing in a semicircle behind him, egging him on, looking for trouble. He was getting to his feet now. He was drunk, he couldn't back down.

It wasn't a good situation.

"Look," I said calmly, "just forget it, OK? It doesn't matter."

He stepped towards me, holding out the pound coin. "You call this *money*?"

I sighed. "I don't want any trouble."

"You want this?" he said, holding out the coin to me.

I didn't say anything.

"You want it? Here . . ." He lobbed the coin into a puddle. "It's yours. Now pick it up."

I looked at him.

He smiled. "Did you hear what I said?"

I glanced behind him at the others. They were quiet, tensed, waiting for it to start.

"Hey," said the drunk.

I looked at him again.

He moved closer, grinning. "I said pick it up, wanker."

It was beyond words now. The line had been crossed. There was only one thing to do. So I did it. I unclipped my guitar strap and moved towards the puddle, holding the guitar by the neck. I heard a snigger, an arrogant snort, then I spun round and hammered my guitar into the drunk guy's head. It made a pretty good sound—a big hollow *boing*—but I don't think it hurt him that much. If he hadn't been drunk he probably wouldn't have fallen over. But he was drunk, and he did fall over, and that was too much for his mates. They all piled in and kicked the shit out of me.

It's late evening now. I couldn't get back to sleep after the whistling episode so I spent a while just walking around, thinking and looking, looking and thinking. There's got to be some way of getting out of here, but I still can't see it.

While I was walking around, Anja and Bird were talking together at the dining table. I heard Bird telling Anja that the police were looking for her. They'd found her car, searched the flat where she'd been abducted, checked the phone records where she worked, etc.

"And?" said Anja.

"Last I heard they didn't seem to be getting anywhere."

Anja shook her head. "Useless bastards."

I carried on wandering around for a while and then I went back to my room.

And here I am.

I've been thinking about Dad, trying to imagine him at one of those press conferences you get when a kid goes missing. The room full of journalists and TV reporters, the cameras, the microphones, the parents (or parent) flanked by serious-looking policemen. The parent/s looking stern, trying not to cry, trying to stay calm. The mother/father's lip quivering as she/he reads out a statement appealing for information . . .

Then I suddenly realized—Dad won't know that I'm missing. Of *course* he won't know. I've already been gone for five months. The only people likely to miss me are Lugless and Bob, Windsor Jack, a few other lowlifes, and they're hardly going to lose any sleep over it. On the street, people come and go all the time. Nothing lasts, no one stays around for long. They might have wondered where I was for a day or so, but after that they would have just nicked all my stuff—blankets, guitar case—and forgotten all about me.

Dad thinks I'm safe. I sent him a letter a couple of days after I left. *I'm all right*, I told him. *I've got money. I'm staying with friends. Please don't call the police. I'll come back when I'm ready. Love Linus.*

I sometimes wonder what Dad thought when he read it. I imagine his face as he opens the envelope. His mouth twitching beneath his grey moustache, his eyes squinting as he unfolds the paper and reads the letter. I wonder if he thought, *Yeah, well, maybe it'll do him some good. Teach him to appreciate what he's got.* Or did he think, *Shit, what's the matter with him? Stupid kid.* Or maybe he just thought...

I don't know.

My brain is spilling over at the moment.

I don't know what to think about anything.

I realize that I haven't fully explained myself yet. I haven't told you what you might (or might not) want to know—my history, my story, the details of my life. But you have to look at things from my point of view. You have to understand what you are to me.

To me, at the moment, you're just a piece of paper. At best, a mirror. At worst, a means to an end. The truth is, all I'm doing is talking to myself. I'm talking to Linus Weems. And I know everything there is to know about him. I know what he's done and what he thinks and what his secrets are. So I don't *need* to explain anything. I don't *need* to tell his story.

I don't *want* to tell it.

I'm sick of it.

11:45 p.m.

I've just been to the bathroom. Arse- and belly-wise, everything seems back to normal.

68

On the way back to my room I saw Anja and Bird again. They were still sitting at the dining table, still talking. They must have been at it all night. Anja had cleaned up her hair and Bird had taken off his jacket and tie. His shirt sleeves were neatly rolled up and he was making those infuriating hand gestures that business people make all the time—pointing, chopping, open-palmed questions. Yuh yuh yuh? Anja was leaning forward with her legs crossed, nodding sincerely at all the right moments, flicking at her hair.

They didn't acknowledge me.

One more thing before I leave it for tonight. Bird said the man got him when he was coming home from work yesterday evening. But, as far as I'm aware, yesterday was a Sunday.

What does that mean?

1) Bird works on Sundays? Unlikely.
2) Bird's lying? Possible.
3) I've got the days mixed up. More than likely.

That's all.

Tuesday (?), 7 February

We've had a meeting.

Anja and Bird announced it. 10:00 a.m. At the dining table. This is how it started:

BIRD (opening his notebook): Is everybody ready? Fred?

FRED (staring at the ceiling, picking burnt skin from his lips): Yeah, what?

BIRD: Are you ready?

FRED: Ready for what?

BIRD: We need to talk. All of us.

FRED (grinning): Right, go on then.

BIRD (looking round the table): OK, let's start by finding out who we all are. I'll set the ball rolling. My name's Will Bird. I'm 38 years old. I was born in Southend and I moved to Chelmsford ten years ago. I share a house with my partner, Lucy, a call-centre manager. I've been a management consultant for eight years, mostly in the banking industry. Before that I worked in customer service training. In my spare time I enjoy paintball games and tinkering with radio-controlled cars. Linus?

ME: What?

BIRD: Tell us about yourself.

ME: Why?

BIRD: Communication, trust—

ME: Trust?

ANJA (to me): Listen to him. He's trying to help.

BIRD (smiling at her): Thank you. (Turning to me with a fake smile) Hey, come on, we have to work together, Linus. We have to pool our resources.

ME: *Hey*, I know.

BIRD: We need spirit, determination, solidarity—

ME: What we need is a way out of here.

FRED: Fucking right.

ANJA: *Christ!*

FRED (glaring at her): What's the matter with you?

ANJA: Nothing.

FRED: Yeah, fucking nothing. Tell me about it. You and your fucking nothing. Ever since you got here all you've done is sit around all day on your tight little arse doing fuck all, then this fat ponce comes along and all of a sudden you're up for it.

BIRD: Now just a minute—

FRED (giving him a threatening look): Yeah?

ANJA (sneering): Oh, that's right. Why don't you hit him with a saucepan?

FRED: At least I'm trying.

ANJA: You can say that again.

FRED: Fuck you.

BIRD (hitting the table): That's *enough*!

FRED: Fuck you too, fat stuff.

Then Jenny started crying.

We took a break.

Anja and Bird went off down the corridor and the rest of us went into the kitchen. While Jenny washed her face and dried her tears, I made some tea and talked quietly to Fred.

"You're frightening Jenny," I told him. "Keep it down a bit. And go easy on the swearing. She's only a kid."

"Kids don't give a shit about swearing."

"Some of them do."

"Yeah, well . . ."

"You're scaring her."

"It's not my fault. It's them, Bird and Anja, they're doing my head in. All this *meetings* shit—"

"Yeah, I know. I don't like it either. But getting all worked up about it isn't going to help, is it?"

He looked at me, his eyes cold with violence.

"You know what I could do to them?" he said.

"All sorts, I imagine."

"You'd be surprised."

An intimate silence hung in the air for a moment. Dirty and hard. I couldn't break it. Whatever words I wanted to say were stuck in the back of my throat. It was all I could do to keep looking at Fred. His great stone head filled the room with unspoken menace.

Then, all at once, his eyes twinkled and his mouth broke into a grin and he leaned across the table and clumped me on the shoulder.

"You know what our trouble is?" he said.

"What?"

"You and me . . . we've both been fucked right from the start."

My home is a big house in the country. It's got six bedrooms, three bathrooms, three reception rooms, a wine cellar, a library, riding stables, a croquet lawn, and a swimming pool. My dad owns three cars. We have another house in California and a villa in the Algarve. And from the age of twelve I've had the best education money can buy.

Yeah, Fred, you're right: fucked from the start.

After half an hour we tried the meeting again. This time we stuck to the basics.

Who, or what, is our abductor?

A psycho.

A pervert.

A people collector.

What does he want?

To watch us.

To kill us.

To keep us as pets.

Where are we?

In a basement.

A cellar.

Somewhere near London?

Somewhere in Essex?

What are we going to do?

Survive.

Escape.

How are we going to survive?

Eat.

Drink.

Keep ourselves clean.
Stay calm.
Get organized.
How do we get organized?

The way we get organized, apparently, is by drawing up a schedule of duties. Which has now been done. So, from now on:

One of us takes charge of the shopping list, logging requests throughout the day, thinking about what else we need, then writing the list and making sure it's in the lift by nine o'clock each evening.

One of us does the washing-up and general cleaning. Any rubbish, put it in a bin liner and put it in the lift. (Put bin liners on the shopping list.)

One of us waits for the lift each morning, collects the shopping, and puts it away.

And one of us cooks. Twice a day. Nine-thirty and six-thirty. If you want anything else to eat at any other time, you have to get it yourself.

We take it in turns, a system, different duties every day.

Another question we tried to discuss at the meeting was How Do We Get Out Of Here? And it was at this point that the meeting went very quiet, and one by one we all looked up at the grille in the ceiling. It looked back at us, mocking our silence with its cold white eye. All-seeing, all-hearing.

Fred broke the silence. "How can we get out of here if he's watching us all the time? We can't even *talk* about escaping."

"You're sure they're cameras?" Bird said.

I nodded. "And microphones."

"And you can't cover them up?"

"What do you think this is?" Fred said, indicating his burnt face. "Sunburn?"

"Hmm," muttered Bird, scribbling something in his notebook.

"Give me that," I said to him.

"What?"

"Your notebook."

"I'm keeping notes of the meeting—"

"Just give it here a second."

He reluctantly passed it over.

"Pen?"

He passed me his pen.

I shielded the page with my hand and wrote: *We've all got a notebook. Keep your back to the cameras, write down any escape ideas, bring them to the table at 10 each night. We can discuss.*

Then I passed the notebook around. When everyone had read it, I said, "OK?"

It was OK.

I said to Bird, "Have you kept a written record of the whole meeting?"

"Of course."

I nodded. "Right, well, there's one more person to come. It'll be easier if you just show him or her your notes rather than having to go over everything again."

"What do you mean, one more person to come?" asked Anja.

"It's pretty obvious, isn't it? There are six rooms down here. Six plates, six cups . . . there's six of everything. But only five of us. There must be one more to come."

Wednesday, 8 February

A long day.

Nothing happens.

We eat, we drink, we stay calm, we get organized. We all look terrible. Pale, drained, haunted. Anja is developing an unbalanced stare. When she's not in her room she walks around looking busy all the time, but her eyes are permanently unfocused, like a caged bear at the zoo. Bird can't keep his eyes off her. He keeps scratching his groin and rubbing his face. Although he's only been here a short while he's already got a thick growth of stubble on his chin. All over his face, in fact. He's a hairy man is Mr. Bird. Fred's beard is longer but stragglier, a bit like Shaggy's beard. You know, Shaggy from *Scooby-Doo*. Not that Fred looks anything like Shaggy. He's more like the Hulk (without the green skin). Imagine the Hulk (without the green skin) with Shaggy's beard and junkie eyes and tattoos all over his body—that's what Fred looks like.

I don't know what I look like. I don't really care. You don't get any points for looking good down here. I *feel* pretty scummy though, and that's not nice. No matter how many times I wash, my skin still feels dirty and clammy, like the dirt is underneath the skin. My head itches too.

The whole thing stinks.

I haven't had a chance to talk to Bird about what day it was when he was abducted. Actually, that's a lie. I've had plenty of chances to talk to him, I just don't want to. As you've probably guessed, I don't like him. He creeps me out. And anyway, it doesn't really matter what day it was. If he's lying, he's lying. There's nothing I can do about that. And if he's not lying, and I've lost a day... well, so what? Who cares what day it is?

6:30 p.m.

Time for tea.

Yippee.

10:30 p.m.

We've just had our first evening meeting. As it was my suggestion, I had the pleasure of collecting everyone's notebooks and reading their escape ideas. Jenny was asleep, so there were only the four of us. Four people. Four pages.

Apart from a neat little heading—*ESCAPE*—Anja's page was blank.

Bird had written—*Dig??? Communicate*

Fred had suggested—*Fire, note down toilet*

And I'd written—*Distraction. Distract him, hide someone in lift. How? Who?*

"Dig?" I said to Bird. "We're in a bloody basement. We're underground. Where the hell are we going to dig to?"

"*Shhh!*" he hissed, pointing at the ceiling.

"Dig," I muttered, shaking my head.

"It was only a thought," Bird said defensively. "I was only, you know, brainstorming."

"You call that a *brainstorm*?"

Fred laughed.

Bird blushed. "All right, maybe it's not such a good idea. But what about the other one? Communication. Why don't we try talking to him?"

"You think he'll listen?" I said.

"We won't know unless we try."

"I already have. I didn't get very far."

"Maybe you didn't do it properly. Communication is a delicate business. It's not just a question of sending a message, you have to think about *how* the message is sent."

"Oh, right," I said, pretending to think about it.

"Content needs context," he said.

"Of course it does."

He squinted at me. "Are you taking the piss?"

"No, I was just thinking. Maybe we could ask him for a laptop and then send him an email. Or better still, a text. Ask him for a mobile phone, ask him for his number, then text him a message. Do you think that might do it?"

Bird gave me an exasperated look. "What's the matter with you? Can't you take *anything* seriously?"

"You started it."

He sighed and shook his head, tutting at me like I was an idiot child. I don't blame him really. It was a pretty childish thing to say. But I am a child, remember. I'm allowed to say childish things. It's my job. And anyway, he *did* start it.

He was sulking now.

I shuffled through the rest of the notebooks and picked out Fred's. I wasn't sure what he meant by *fire*, but the other idea sounded promising. I wrote down—*Fire's too dangerous, but work on the message-down-the-toilet idea*—and then passed

78

the notebook around. Anja read it, shrugged, and passed it to Bird. Mr. Sulky. I didn't think he'd even bother to read it, but to his credit he took the notebook and studied the message, then wrote something down and passed it back to me.

I glanced at him for a moment, feeling a tiny bit guilty, then I looked at the page. He'd written—*We'd need a waterproof container, something that floats, small plastic bottle?*

"Yeah," I said. "Good idea. Let's think about it."

Finally I passed my idea around, the one about hiding in the lift.

I said, "I haven't figured out all the details yet, but I'm working on it."

I got a couple of shrugs and a raised eyebrow from Fred.

And that was about it.

I ought to feel more hopeful, I suppose. At least we're talking, thinking, doing *something*. We're beginning to work together, and that's good. Because, when you get right down to it, it's us against him. The Man Upstairs. Mister Crazy. The Man With No Name. Call him what you like. Whoever He is, He holds all the cards. He's got us right where He wants us. All we can do is try to make the most of what little we've got.

And what *have* we got?

Well, I suppose we've got the advantage of numbers. We're five and He's one. Five brains against one. And, if I'm right, it should soon be six. Six against one. Even better. Six brains against one. It's not much, I know. I mean, they're pretty mushy brains, and they're probably going to get even mushier if we stay here much longer. But five or six mushy brains working together is a lot better than five or six mushy brains working on their own. Do you see what I mean? It's like an ant thing. You know, like

79

the difference between an individual ant and an ant colony. An ant on its own can't do much, but when it gets together with all its ant-colleagues it can do almost anything. It can build cities, capture slaves, and create underground gardens. It can rampage through the jungle eating everything in sight. That's what we have to do, only on a slightly smaller scale.

This evening was a start. It wasn't the greatest of starts, but at least it was a start. We're getting there. We're improving our chances of getting out. Not a lot, I admit. I mean, we're not ready for any rampaging just yet. But not a lot is a lot better than nothing.

So, yeah, I ought to be feeling more hopeful. I ought to be feeling more optimistic, more positive.

That's how I *ought* to be feeling.

The trouble is, deep down, I can't help feeling it's all a waste of time.

Thursday, 9 February

I was right, number six arrived this morning.

It was my turn to meet the lift. I was standing in the corridor with a bag of rubbish in my hand, pondering my idea about escaping in the lift, when down it came, opened up, and there he was.

His name's Russell Lansing.

I know him. At least, I know who he is. I've seen his photograph in the newspapers and on the back of his book, *Time and Stuff: Natural Philosophy in the 21st Century.*

He was in the wheelchair, tied and gagged, but he was awake. His eyes were open. Scared, red and watery, but open. I wheeled him out and gently peeled the tape from his mouth.

"Thank you," he gasped. "Where am I?"

I started untying him. As I worked on the knots I explained as much as I could—the five of us, the lift, the food, the cameras and microphones. It all sounded pretty weird. It's strange how you can get used to something and not realize how peculiar it is until you start talking about it. I know I've been talking to you for the last few weeks, but that's different. That's silent talking. This was *real* talking.

Russell listened patiently as I told him the story, not saying anything until I'd finished.

Then all he said was, "I see."

Very calm.

"Are you all right?" I asked him.

He nodded, rubbing his wrists and looking around. "Drugged, I believe. No physical injuries." He looked at me. "How long have you been here?"

"Nearly two weeks."

"Two *weeks*?"

"Seems a lot longer."

"I'll bet it does." He rubbed his eyes. "Is there a bathroom I can use? I must have been sitting in this chair for about four hours."

"Yeah. Can you walk?"

"I think so."

He tried getting out of the chair, but halfway up he winced painfully and closed his eyes, then sat back down again and took a couple of deep breaths.

"Perhaps not," he said.

"No problem."

I wheeled him down the corridor to the bathroom. As we went, his eyes never stopped moving, studying the walls, the ceiling, the doors, the floor. Everything.

"What's behind these doors?" he asked.

"Rooms."

"Is that where the others are?"

"They'll be sleeping," I told him. "We tend to stay in bed a lot. They'll be up soon for breakfast."

"Breakfast?"

"We're very civilized."

He smiled.

I said, "You're Russell Lansing, aren't you?"

"I am indeed."

"I'm Linus Weems."

"Weems?"

I nodded. "I've read your book."

"Oh, yes?"

"I really liked it."

"Thank you."

I didn't know what else to say. I felt a bit embarrassed, to tell you the truth. A bit sappy, like a little kid talking to his favourite pop star. I was glad the others weren't around. Despite the embarrassment it was a nice little moment, and I wanted it all to myself. I'd found him. I knew who he was. I'd read his book. He was *mine*.

"Here we are," I said. "This is the bathroom. Can you make it from here?"

"I think so."

I helped him out of the chair.

"There's a sheet on the back of the door," I said. "To hide yourself from the camera."

"There's a camera in the *bathroom*?"

I nodded. "If you slip the sheet over your head he can't see you."

"Right. Well, thank you."

I watched him walk slowly into the bathroom and shut the door. He's old, nearly seventy I'd guess. His black skin is dull and grey and his hair is all brittle and white. I remember reading somewhere that he does a lot of work with AIDS charities, that he has the disease himself, that he's dying.

I can believe that.

Over breakfast he told us all what had happened.

"It was my own fault," he said. "I met a fellow in a bar. I let him buy me a few drinks, and then I rather foolishly agreed to accompany him home. I think I did anyway. I was rather befuddled at the time."

Fred laughed. "Befuddled?"

Russell held his hand out, palm upwards. He raised it slowly, paused, then turned it over and brought it down flat on the kitchen table.

Fred grinned.

I wasn't sure what he was grinning at, but I joined him anyway. It felt like the right thing to do. It felt good. Then I looked round the table at the others and my smile faded. Anja and Bird had been giving Russell funny looks ever since I'd introduced him. I didn't know why, and I didn't much care. But the way they were looking at each other now, shaking their heads and exchanging disapproving glances, it really bugged me for some reason.

"Something on your mind?" I asked Bird.

He looked at me, sniffed, then turned to Russell. "This man you met in the bar," he said coldly. "Did you get a close look at him?"

"Close enough."

"What was he like?"

Russell gave it some thought. After a while he said, "Charming . . . manipulative . . . persuasive . . . intelligent . . . endearingly bland. In hindsight, a classic psychopath."

"Description?"

"Middle-aged, dark hair, about five feet ten inches tall. Well built, but not overly muscular. Strong hands. Clean-shaven.

Lightly tinted spectacles. Charcoal suit, white shirt, burgundy tie. Black slip-on shoes, burgundy socks."

Bird looked sceptical. "You remember all that?"

"I'm a physicist. I'm trained to observe."

"Oh, right," Bird scoffed. "*That's* what you were doing, was it? Hanging round bars *observing* other men."

Russell looked at him. "I'm gay, Mr. Bird. Is that a problem?"

"No . . . no, of course not. I was just saying . . . "

Fred let out a snort of laughter. "Jesus! You're black *and* you're bent?"

It wasn't the most subtle way of putting it, and I was half-expecting Russell to lose his temper and storm off or something, but he didn't seem to mind at all. He just looked at Fred and smiled. Fred smiled back at him. Then, without a word, Russell put his hand to his eye, lowered his head, and dug around with his fingers. After a moment he looked up again and held out his hand. Where his eye had been there was now just an empty socket, and in his hand there was a smooth glass bauble.

"Not only black and bent, my friend," he said to Fred, "but one-eyed to boot."

Late evening.

Mixed emotions.

I like Russell. I like his calm, his insight, his sadness. I like his humour. I like the way he accepts things. It gives us balance. It gives *me* balance. I'm not sure why. It's probably got something to do with him being smart. He's a very clever man, Russell. He knows stuff. And I like that. I like it because I'm smart too, and we all like things that remind us of ourselves. I'm not saying I'm a genius or anything. I mean, I don't know as much as Russell, obviously. In fact, there's plenty of stuff I don't know the first thing about. But I'm well educated. I've been taught how to think. So even if I don't know the facts about something I can usually work out how to think about it. And that's what being smart is—knowing how to think. Facts are all well and good, but they don't mean anything if you don't know what to do with them.

Anyway, I'm smart. That's all I'm saying. I feel an affinity with Russell because I'm smart. It's no big deal. I'm not bragging or anything. It's just what I am. We're all something. I'm smart. Fred's strong. Jenny's kind. Anja's beautiful. Bird's . . . fat. We all have our qualities, and none of them are any better or worse than the others. They're just different.

At this evening's meeting Russell didn't have a lot to say. None of us did. There were no new ideas, no suggestions, no eurekas. Bird seemed preoccupied with something and hardly said a word. Anja had a headache and retired to her room. Even Fred seemed unnaturally quiet. The only one who had anything constructive to say was Jenny. When I showed her the escape ideas from last night she quickly looked over the pages, moving her lips as she read, then she jabbed her finger at my distraction idea and said, "That one. The rest are useless."

I couldn't help smiling. "What about Fred's?"

"Which one's that?"

I showed her the idea about putting a message down the toilet.

She read it again, looked at Fred, then giggled.

"What?" he said. "It's a *good* idea."

"It won't work—" she started to say.

"Shh," I said. "Write it down. Here." I passed her a pen and a piece of paper.

She bent low to the table and shielded the page with her arm. Her tongue poked out from her lips as she wrote: *What will the mesage say? We don't know anything. We don't know where we are or anything. Whats the point of writing a mesage when we don't know what to write?*

I showed it to the others.

We looked at each other.

"Shit," said Fred. "She's right."

Jenny smiled proudly.

After the meeting Russell said he'd like a word with me. I made some coffee and took it into his room. He's in room six. As I was shutting the door Bird passed by, heading down the corridor towards his room, number four.

"Watch yourself in there," he smirked.

I ignored him and shut the door. When I turned round, Russell was lowering himself gingerly to the bed. He looked to be in some pain.

"Are you all right?" I asked.

"It's nothing," he said, indicating the chair. "Please, sit down."

I sat.

Russell sipped his coffee and stared at the grille in the ceiling. "Damnable thing," he said eventually.

"What, the camera?"

"All of it. Everything. This place . . . all of you . . . that poor little girl . . ." His voice trailed off and he shook his head. "I saw her parents on television. It's all very disturbing."

I didn't say anything. I didn't feel the need to say anything. I just sat there. It was quiet. The walls hummed. The time passed. After a while Russell looked up and cocked his head.

"That humming sound, is it always there?"

I nodded.

He listened. He looked at the grille in the ceiling, then put his hand against the wall.

"Small generator," he said, almost to himself. "Four-cylinder, diesel engine." He took his hand away and looked at me. "This is quite an operation."

"You think so?"

He looked around, nodding. "Most impressive. It must have taken an awful lot of time and money."

"What do you think this place is?" I asked him. "A basement? Do you think we can get out? What do you think—?"

"Whoa," he said gently, holding up a hand.

"Sorry. You must be tired."

He smiled. "I'm always tired. I'm old." He sipped his coffee. "I'll have a good look round tomorrow, and we'll see what we're up against. Perhaps you'd like to give me the guided tour?"

"My pleasure."

We lapsed into silence again.

After a while the silence was broken by a faint sobbing sound from the room next door. Anja. Her cries were muffled, as if she had her head buried in a pillow.

Russell cleared his throat. "The young lady..."

"Anja."

"Anja, yes. Is she involved with Mr. Bird?"

"Involved?"

"I heard them talking earlier on. The walls are quite thin. He was in her room."

"They spend a lot of time together."

He nodded thoughtfully. "Perhaps more than Anja wants."

"What do you mean?"

He shrugged. "She asked him to leave her alone. She sounded rather upset."

"Probably just frayed nerves," I said. "This place can get to you."

"I can imagine."

A strange thing happened then. His good eye started blinking, slowly and steadily, and then his face stilled and his eye glazed over and he just sat there staring into space. After a while his head began to sag, as if he was falling asleep. It just hung there, bowed to his chest. I moved my chair, squeaking it on the floor, and then I noisily cleared my throat a couple of times. But he didn't seem to hear me. I started worrying that he'd passed out or something. I was just about to get up and give him a nudge on the arm when his head gave a little jerk and he suddenly straightened up, his eye wide open.

"Uh?" he said. "What's ...? What?"

"Mr. Lansing?"

He looked at me. Confusion showed briefly on his face, and then it suddenly cleared again and he smiled. "Linus," he said. "Linus Weems."

"That's right."

"Charlie Weems's son."

I stared at him.

"I'm right, aren't I?" he said. "You're Charlie Weems's son?"

"How do you know that?"

"Well, Weems is quite an unusual surname, isn't it? And I remember reading an article about your father a few years ago in which he mentioned a teenage son. I also remember reading somewhere that your father is a huge fan of the *Peanuts* cartoons, and I seem to recall that Charlie Brown's best friend was a character called Linus van Pelt." He smiled at me. "I'm not really a great admirer of the Gribbles, but I've always loved cartoons and comic strips, and I think your father's earlier work is up there with the very best."

Some people have the ability to get you talking. They can get you telling stuff that you wouldn't normally share with anyone else. Russell is like that. I don't know how he does it. He doesn't really do anything special, he just sits there, asking the odd question and listening patiently. There's a peacefulness about him that brings things out.

He certainly got me talking.

⌐ I didn't mean to start telling him everything about my dad, but once I'd told him that he was right, that I *am* Charlie Weems's son, and that Dad's earlier work *is* really good, and the Gribbles *are* really crap, and that Dad *did* name me after the character in the *Peanuts* cartoons, I just couldn't seem to stop talking.

"I've never forgiven him for calling me Linus," I admitted. "It's such a *stupid* name."

"It could have been worse," Russell said. "He could have called you Snoopy."

"Well, yeah, but at least everyone's heard of Snoopy. Most of the kids I know don't have a clue who Linus van Pelt is. They just think I've got a really stupid name."

Russell smiled sympathetically. "Linus is the one with the security blanket, isn't he? The little kid who believes in the Great Pumpkin?"

"Yeah."

We talked a bit about Dad's cartoons then. They're actually nothing like the *Peanuts* cartoons. They're a lot darker, a lot more unsettling, and they're not really suitable for young kids. A lot of people compare them to Gary Larson's *Far Side* stuff, and I suppose they're a bit like that. A bit surreal, a bit bizarre. But if you ask other cartoonists to describe my dad's stuff, most of them will compare it to the work of a man called Bernard Kliban, who very few people have ever heard of . . .

Which was pretty much my dad's situation until the Gribbles took off.

"Is it true that before the TV series he never made any money from his cartoons?" Russell asked.

"He made a bit," I said. "But not very much. Most of his money came from the stuff he got published in magazines, which wasn't a lot."

"What about his books?"

"Nobody bought them."

"So how did you manage?"

"My mum had a job. She was a lawyer. That's how she met Dad in the first place. He was one of her clients." I looked at Russell. "Dad got done for drugs, and Mum helped to keep him out of prison."

Russell smiled. "And then they fell in love and got married?"

"Yeah, I suppose so. Although . . . well, I was only little when Mum was around so it's hard to remember anything very clearly, but I know they used to argue quite a lot, shouting and screaming at each other like maniacs. Mum was always nagging at Dad to get a proper job. She'd get really angry sometimes, telling him that she was fed up with him sponging off her all the time.

I don't know if she meant it or not, but there was no doubt that Dad *was* dependent on her for money. That's partly why everything got so bad when she died . . . "

— I was nine years old when my mum died.

She got ill, started staying in bed a lot. Her room smelled bad. She went into hospital and died.

Dad cried a lot and stayed drunk for days at a time.

I can't think about it.

Can't . . .

Don't want to.

"Dad had to start selling stuff eventually," I told Russell. "The car, Mum's jewellery, whatever there was. He sold it all. And we still didn't have any money. It got so bad that he even began looking for a job, a real job, something that would actually bring in some money every week."

"Did he find one?"

I smiled. "All he's ever done is draw cartoons. He doesn't know how to do anything else. He's totally unpresentable, he doesn't like people, he's rude, he takes drugs, he drinks too much . . . "

"Not the ideal employee then?"

I laughed. "Not really."

"So what happened?"

The Gribbles happened, for God's sake.

The Gribbles.

You've probably never heard of them. I mean, they're massive in most parts of the world, especially in the Far East, but for some reason they've never really caught on in the UK. Dad's original picture book—called simply *The Gribbles*—was published here but it probably only sold about twenty copies. Not that Dad cared. He never wanted to do the book in the first place. He didn't even like the Gribbles. They were just something he'd drawn one day when he was bored, a few sketched doodles at the bottom of a page. He'd never meant them to be anything. But his publisher happened to notice the sketches when Dad was showing her something else, and she thought they'd make good characters for a children's picture book.

"I don't *do* children's picture books," Dad told her.

"I can't pay you for your other stuff, Charlie," she told him. "I'm sorry, but nobody wants it."

Dad sighed. "So how much can you give me for the Gribbles?"

Not much, was the answer. But that was enough for Dad. He went to work on the Gribbles, fleshing out the sketches until he had his basic character, which in effect was just a big lumpy head with stubby little arms and legs, and then he drew about half a dozen different versions, gave each of them a different colour, came up with a few little adventures for them, and that was pretty much it.

The Gribbles.

They look a bit like this:

All I can really remember about the original book is that the colour of each Gribble was supposed to represent its personality. So Blue Gribble was sad, Red Gribble was excitable, Black Gribble was . . .

I can't remember what Black Gribble was. Evil, probably. Or maybe depressed?

I can't remember.

Anyway, the book came out, no one bought it, and the Gribbles sank without a trace. And then, just at the point when everything seemed utterly hopeless, Dad's agent rang to say that a Japanese TV company had bought the rights to the book and they were making a cartoon series based on the characters.

And that's how Dad became rich beyond his dreams. The TV series was a huge hit in Japan, and within a year or so it had been sold to almost every country in the world, and the money just started pouring in. And it's carried on pouring in ever since. Dad even gets a cut of all the merchandising—the Gribble dolls, the Gribble lunchboxes, the Gribble pencil cases. He makes a fortune from that kind of crap.

And, of course, he loved it at first. He bought all the stuff you're supposed to buy when you're rich—the big house in the country, the beach house in Santa Monica, the villa, the cars, a boat . . . vast amounts of drink and drugs . . . he could buy whatever he wanted. And he did. But after a while (and after he'd stuffed so much cocaine up his nose that he was almost permanently up in the clouds) he began to realize (or at least tell himself) that money alone wasn't enough, and that what he really wanted, above all else, was respect. He wanted to be taken seriously. He wanted to be known as an artist, as someone with something to say. He didn't want to be remembered as the man who created the Gribbles.

(An interviewer once asked him if he was proud of them. "*Proud* of the Gribbles?" Dad snorted. "I *despise* the fucking things.")

And now, the more money the Gribbles make for him, the more bitter and twisted he becomes. It eats away at him every day. It drives him crazy. And that's why he can't stop chasing around all over the world, trying to get his "projects' up and running—animated films, graphic novels, experimental CGI stuff. The kind of stuff that he hopes will give him the respect he thinks he deserves. And that's why I've had to put up with too many years of boarding school, too many years of cold grey walls and twisted teachers and snotty kids with savage minds . . .

"It got to the point where I just couldn't stand it any more," I told Russell. "It was driving me mad. I mean, it probably wouldn't have been so bad if I'd had a home to go to at the end of the day, but I didn't. I had to *live* there. I had to be there *all* the time. Day in, day out, night after night, having to put up with the same old crap—the stupid jokes about my name, the nasty little comments—"

"What kind of comments?" Russell said. "If you don't mind me asking."

"Nothing much really. Just the usual small-minded shit, you know. The kind of stuff you get when you don't fit in—you're some kind of weirdo, or you must be gay or something . . ." I looked at Russell, suddenly embarrassed. "Sorry," I said quickly. "I didn't mean—"

"It's perfectly all right," he said, smiling. "I know exactly what you mean. Life can be hard when you don't fit in."

I nodded. "It wasn't even that bad really. You know, I didn't get beaten up or anything, and most of the time I didn't really care what the other kids thought of me anyway. But I just couldn't stand having to be with them all the time. Watching them eat, watching them wash. Hearing them belch and fart. Smelling their smells. It was a ridiculous way to live. Everything about it just stank." I sighed. "You know that horrible smell of someone else's shit? It was like that, *all* the time."

"So," Russell said, "you ran away?"

"Well, I didn't exactly *run*."

"But you left school. You left home."

I nodded again. "Dad drove me back to school after the summer holidays. He dropped me off, I waved him goodbye, and then I just walked into town and got on a train to London. That was just over five months ago. I've been living on the streets ever since."

"And how has that been?"

I shrugged. "It's all right."

He smiled. "Any less smelly?"

"Not really. But at least you can get away from it."

"Where do you sleep?"

"Anywhere. Mostly around Liverpool Street."

"Hostels?"

"No, I tried one once. It was worse than school. It's best to stick to the streets. There's plenty of places if you know where to look. Doorways, abandoned houses, railway tunnels. It's not as bad as it sounds."

"What do you live on?"

"Busking, begging, handouts. A bit of stealing now and then."

"It must be hard."

"No harder than anything else."

"Do you . . . ? " he hesitated. "Do you take anything to make it easier?"

"You mean drugs?"

He nodded.

"No," I said. "I don't take drugs. I've seen what they can do. I don't want to end up like my dad."

"But there must be a lot of drugs around?"

"There's a lot of everything around."

Russell went quiet again then. He just sat there, staring silently at his shoes. It seemed a reasonable thing to do, so I joined him. They were nice shoes to look at. Like Teddy Boys' shoes. Black suede uppers and thick rubber soles.

After a while he looked up at me and said, "You're a remarkable young man, Linus."

"Why's that?"

"You stick to your guns."

"Do I?"

"Well, you must get offered things all the time. Drink, drugs . . . whatever. And you just say no. I think that's very admirable."

"Not really," I said. "I just don't want to die, that's all."

Now it's late.

I'm tired, exhausted. I haven't talked so much for ages. I don't think I've *ever* talked so much about Dad. I'm absolutely drained. But I can't seem to stop writing.

I feel a long way from everything.

Floating, sad, apprehensive, cold. I wish things were different, but they're not. They never are. They can't be.

I can't get Dad out of my mind. I keep wondering what he's doing right now. I try to picture him at home, in the front room maybe, sipping brandy in front of the fire. Or in the kitchen, at the table, surrounded by the dark oak beams, the sealed brick walls, the copper pans hanging on the wall...

But I can't see it. I can't see anything.

It's all too far away. Too long ago.

Everything is too long ago.

I have hazy memories of being at home with Mum and Dad when I was little, but I don't know if these memories are true or not. They run like bootleg DVDs in the back of my mind, all grainy and jumpy from being copied too many times. I remember Dad making up stories and poems for me, singing me songs, showing me cartoons and pictures in books... but it isn't him, it's just a memory of him.

And Mum...

I don't want to think any more.

I wish I'd asked Russell if he'd heard anything about Dad, if he'd read any recent articles about him or seen any interviews or anything. He does interviews sometimes, trying to promote his latest project. He never talks about the Gribbles though. He doesn't usually talk about his personal life either, but I just thought that maybe if he had been on TV or something he might have mentioned me. You know, a message or something, a plea for information...

But I guess Russell would have told me if he'd heard anything.

It's hard not caring.

Hard enough to make you cry.

Friday, 10 February

Last night I dreamed about Lugless and Pretty Bob. They were at school with me. It was night-time, in the dormitory. Lug and Bob were holding court, telling stories, and all the kids were sitting round listening to them. The strange thing was, I didn't know any of the kids' names. I recognized their faces, but I couldn't put any names to them. Anyway, they were all sitting round with their eyes glued to Lug and Bob as if they were TV stars or something. Pretty Bob was leaning against the wall eating a banana, and Lug was sitting cross-legged on the floor telling how he lost his ear.

"Nah, nah, listen," he was saying. "You know the thing about whatsis? The crow-man, flowers, the painter, Vango—"

"Goff," said Pretty Bob. "Von Goff."

"Right, him. See, what he did, there was this other painter man did jungles and tigers and stuff and Goff din't like him—"

"Gangrene," said Bob.

"Yep, yep, that's him. Goff had a fight with Gangrene and Gangrene shot off Goff's ear. And that's what happened with me. 'Cept it was crayons with me."

"The Terminator's crayons," said Bob.

Lug grinned. "Yeah, the Turnimaker. Whoo, he's a big boy, that one. See, I took his crayons and he ate my ear."

"That's why he don't get no drinks," said Bob. "You ask Lug if he wants a drink, he says, 'No thanks, I got one ear.'"

All the kids started laughing.

And then I got up and said, "That's not what happened."

And everyone looked at me.

I said, "A dog bit him, that's all. That's how Lug lost his ear. A dog bit him."

Everyone's eyes went cold, like I'd ruined everything, and then the scene faded and the view panned out to a small white building standing alone on the top of a hill in the middle of an open prairie. I think it was a farmhouse. It could have been a chapel, but I'm pretty sure it was a farmhouse. Like one of those old-fashioned places you see in Western films, you know? A plain wooden building with a bell tower at one end and a corral out the front. The bell tower was what made me think it might be a chapel, but I'm sure it was a farmhouse.

It was summer. The sky was clear and blue, the prairie grass was whispering softly in a lazy breeze. The corral, if that's what it was, formed a perfect circle bounded by a white picket fence.

And that's where I was sitting. Right in the middle of the corral.

I don't know why I was at this farmhouse, but I'm fairly sure I didn't live there. I don't think anyone lived there. And I don't know where I came from or how I got there either. The dream had no journey. But I have a kind of dream-memory of crossing the prairie and climbing the hill, and I can remember the feel of the long grass brushing softly against me . . .

Anyway, there I was, sitting cross-legged in the dry dirt in the middle of the corral . . . surrounded by a host of furry animals. They were toy animals, stuffed animals, you know the kind of thing. Soft toys with glass eyes and stitched mouths. And they all had the most incredible brightly coloured fur. Vivid yellow, electric blue, fluorescent red . . . orange, lilac, cartoon pink . . .

And they were alive.

They *were* stuffed animals, but they were also alive.

They didn't do very much in the dream, they just sat around in a gently fidgeting circle, murmuring softly to one another, glancing at me every now and then. They were definitely alive though.

There's no doubt about that.

There were about two dozen of them, maybe more. Thirty or so. Monkeys, bears, cows, dogs, tigers, lions, pigs, sheep, penguins, crocodiles, chickens . . . all kinds of animals. They were all about the same size, about the size of a small dog, or a cat, and they all had coats of irresistibly soft and shiny fur, the kind of fur that makes you want to reach out and stroke it.

But I didn't reach out and stroke it.

I didn't stroke the animals.

I didn't have to. All I had to do was sit there and let them smile at me. That's all I had to do. It was wonderful.

I think they loved me.

Simple as that.

I just sat there, they smiled at me, and then after a while the bell rang and it was time to go. And that was it. The farm bell rang when it was time to go back down the hill. The bell rang, I stood up and walked away, down the hill, and the animals' eyes went cold, like I'd ruined everything, and then the dream faded to black.

It doesn't mean anything. Dreams never mean anything. All it means is that everything's the same. School, the street, madmen, beggars, animals, me . . . we're all the same.

We're all interchangeable.

This afternoon I showed Russell around the building. There wasn't really much to show him, but it was still slow going. He tires very easily. His eyes—his *eye*—keeps glazing over and he has to keep sitting down for a rest. So it took a long time, but that didn't matter. We didn't have much else to do. I showed him everything. The lift, the rooms, the walls, the floor, the ceiling, the grilles. And he studied it all with a quiet intensity, asking me questions, touching things, listening, sniffing, making notes, looking at things, all the time nodding quietly and humming to himself.

Afterwards he went into his room to think about things.

An hour later he came out and called us all to the table.

"We're in a reconditioned bunker," he announced. "The walls are constructed of .75-metre concrete strengthened with steel mesh. The roof is at least one metre thick and the foundations are set in about three metres of concrete. The lift shaft is made of tank steel and probably protected with heavy blast walls. Lights, heating, plumbing, and ventilation are powered by a diesel-engine generator system." He paused and looked at the ceiling. "Those grilles were originally part of a filtration system for extracting radioactive material and chemical or biological agents. The system has been adapted to allow gases to be pumped *into* the bunker, and the grilles have been fitted with audio and video surveillance equipment—"

"What's a bunker?" interrupted Jenny.

Russell smiled. "An underground building. Like a bomb shelter. Most of them were built in the early 1950s when the threat of nuclear war became a reality. They were originally intended as command centres for the deployment and firing of our anti-aircraft defences." He gazed around. "Of course, the original building would have been a lot bigger than this. There would have been lots of rooms, a command centre, communication equipment, even different levels. This . . . " He waved his hands, indicating the building. "This is just a small part of the original bunker. Probably the living quarters. The rest of it must have been sealed up or blocked in. That's what I meant by reconditioned. You see—"

Bird yawned loudly.

Russell looked at him. "I take it you find this uninteresting?"

"Well," said Bird, "it doesn't exactly help a lot, does it?"

Russell said nothing.

Bird said, "Hey, don't get me wrong. I'm sure you know what you're talking about, and if I wasn't stuck down here I'm sure I'd find it fascinating. But let me ask you something. All this fancy talk, all this historical bullshit—how's it going to get us out of here?"

Russell didn't answer.

Bird grinned smugly—like the fool who thinks he's outsmarted the professor—and his fat eyes glanced around the table, seeking approval. No one said anything. There wasn't anything to say. Bird took that to mean we agreed with him.

"You *see*?" he said, grinning triumphantly. "You see what I mean?"

I felt like hitting him.

After that the meeting kind of petered out and we all drifted away to sit around doing nothing. A little while later though, I met up with Russell and Fred and we had a little chat about something.

I can't tell you what it was.

It's a secret.

It's evening now. Seven o'clock, eight o'clock, something like that. It'll be dark outside. Dark, cold, probably raining. I expect it's windy too. One of those hard gusty winds that spits the rain against the back of your neck like tiny wet needles. I wouldn't mind some of that right now. A bit of rain, a sharp breeze, the night sky. Stars . . .

Shit.

This is the worst time of day. From about five until midnight. That's when the time *really* drags. I don't know why. It's no less boring than any other time of day, but for some reason it really gets to me. The silence, the whiteness, the emptiness.

Down here the evenings last for ever.

There's not much to do.

I think a lot.

I think of all sorts of things.

You wouldn't believe some of the things I think about. And I'm not going to tell you either. I mean, think about it. If I told you all my thoughts . . . well, imagine that. Think your darkest thoughts, then imagine telling them to a stranger. How does that feel?

Right.

Thinking isn't criminal.

But there's another reason I don't tell you everything, a more practical reason. You see, you are the unknown. You are you, and sometimes you're me, but you're also Him, The Man Upstairs. Or at least you *could* be Him. I'm not saying you are, but I have to bear that possibility in mind. I mean, I do everything I can to keep these words hidden. I don't leave the notebook lying around. I close it when I'm not writing. I always write with my back to the cameras. But there are no guarantees down here. Anything is possible. I have no way of knowing that The Man Upstairs isn't reading my thoughts. I have no way of knowing that He *is* either.

I suppose I could just ask Him.

Hey, Mister, are you reading this? Give me a sign if you are. Knock on the ceiling or something. And by the way, while I've got you on the line, let me tell you something. Let me tell you this: I know that I might die in here. I'm well aware of that. I know that you might kill me. In fact, I think you probably will. But you can't kill my thoughts. Thoughts don't need a body. They don't need air. They don't need food or water or blood. So even if you do kill me, I'll still be thinking of you. Do you understand what I'm saying? I'll be thinking of you until the end of time.

And that's a stone-cold promise.

Think about *that*, Mister.

You think about that.

Saturday, 11 February

Now He's started playing games.

When the lift came down this morning, there was the usual bag of food, plus some cleaning stuff that Jenny had asked for—bottles of disinfectant and bleach—and there was also a large cardboard box. It was one of those packing boxes that supermarkets throw out or leave by the door for putting your shopping in. A big one. All taped up. It was Anja's turn to get the food out of the lift, but we were all there when it came down. We usually are. It's the highlight of the day. Anyway, we got the food out and put the box on the kitchen table and then opened it up.

It contained:

Six bottles of vodka.
Ten packets of cigarettes.
Three disposable lighters.
Several pornographic magazines (of various persuasions).
A syringe.
A metal teaspoon.
A small plastic bag full of brown powder.
Some newspaper clippings.

We all just stood there for a while, staring at all this stuff like fishes studying a worm on a hook, and I felt my heart sinking.

I looked around at the kinds of eyes and faces I've seen a thousand times before—hungry eyes, hungry faces, empty heads saying gimme, gimme, gimme.

I knew what it meant.

I could visualize The Man Upstairs watching us all with a sick grin on His face, thinking to Himself—*Right, let's see you working on that lot together.*

It was a smart move, I'll give Him that. Smart and nasty.

Fred was the first to crack. I somehow knew he would be. He stepped forward and reached for the polythene bag and a bottle of vodka, and then the rest of them jumped in and took the bait. Snap snap snap. Gimme, gimme, gimme. Anja ripped open a packet of cigarettes and scrabbled for a lighter, and Bird grabbed a bottle and twisted off the cap.

"Hold on," I said.

But they weren't listening. Their eyes burned fiercely as they tore open their toys.

I turned to Russell. "Do something."

"What?"

"Stop them."

He shook his head sadly.

I turned back to the table. Bird was taking a slug from the bottle and Fred was dabbing his finger in the polythene bag. I grabbed his arm.

"Don't be stupid," I said. "You've only just got off it."

He brushed my hand away.

"Come on, Fred," I begged. "Please?"

He just stared at me.

"I *need* you," I told him.

"I need *this*."

"Why?"

"Why *anything*? Why not?"

"But—"

He pushed me away, grabbed a magazine and some cigarettes, and marched out of the kitchen. I sighed and looked around. The table was strewn with ripped cellophane and torn paper. Bird had gone. Anja was sitting down, sucking hungrily on a cigarette. She looked up at me with a self-satisfied grin and blew smoke into the air.

"Yeah?" she said nastily. "What are *you* looking at?"

"Nothing."

I've burned the remaining magazines. I was going to burn the cigarettes too, and pour the vodka down the sink, but then I thought—it's not up to me, is it? I can't make choices for other people. We all want and need different things. And besides, if I poured the vodka away and burned the cigarettes I'd probably get beaten up.

The newspaper clippings were mostly about Jenny's disappearance. There were a couple about Anja, and one about Bird, but the rest were all about Jenny. There were photographs of her, of her parents, of the street where she went missing. There were articles, theories, suppositions, details of various suspects the police had interviewed, words of outrage from politicians and journalists.

I didn't let Jenny see them.

It would only have upset her.

I burned them all.

Then I went to my room and screamed silently at the walls.

It's all about games. He's playing His and we're playing ours. His involves giving us what we think we want—our vices—or what He thinks will damage us—our weaknesses—and then seeing what happens. I suppose it's a bit like one of those artificial-life computer games. You know, the kinds of games that let you play God. Yeah, I can see Him liking that. He's bound to be that kind of person. An only child, probably. The sort of kid who spent all his time on his own, setting light to ants and pulling the legs off spiders.

Yeah, I can see that.

10:00 p.m.

Games.

I've spent most of the night playing word games with Jenny and Russell. Tennis Elbow, Hangman, stuff like that. I wasn't really in the mood for it, but I didn't want to leave Jenny on her own. There's a nasty feeling in the air tonight. Fred's whacked out of his head in his room. Anja's sobbing drunk. And Bird's been stomping around shouting like a lunatic all night.

It's nothing to worry about really, but it's probably pretty scary for a little kid.

So that's why we've been playing games. It helps to pass the time, and it takes Jenny's mind off things.

Mine too, I suppose.

Russell's really good with Jenny. He's got this "twinkly old man" thing about him, like he's wise and pleasantly stupid at the same time. I know it's only an act, and I think Jenny does too, but it's still pretty good.

Like when Jenny asked him what he was.

"I'm a natural philosopher," he told her.

"What's that?"

"A sort of physicist. I ask questions about the world, and then I try to answer them."

"What sort of questions?"

"All sorts, but mostly the kinds of questions we forget about asking when we grow up. Like why the sky is blue, why space is black, why stars shine, why we have two eyes."

Jenny smiled. "Why *do* we have two eyes?"

Russell plucked a loose button from his shirt and placed it on the bed about half a metre from Jenny. "Close one eye," he told her, "then touch the button with your finger."

Jenny looked at him.

"Go on," he said.

She closed one eye and reached out to touch the button. Her finger started wobbling, she frowned, then jabbed at the bed, missing the button by a couple of centimetres.

"Hey," she said, opening her eye.

Russell smiled. "That's why we have two eyes, to stop us *Hey*ing."

The night goes on. It's just me and Jenny now. Russell's face started looking a bit pale about half an hour ago, then his head started nodding and his eyes began to close. I gave him a nudge and told him to go back to his room and go to bed.

"Will you be all right?" he said.

"No trouble."

"Are you sure?"

"Yeah, go on."

He went.

So here I am, sitting with my back to the door, talking to myself again. Jenny's in bed with the sheets pulled up over her head, trying to sleep. Outside, Bird is still stomping around, shouting his drunken mouth off.

It's one of those nights.

I've been here before. Sitting in my room listening to Dad going crazy about something. Nights at boarding school, stupid stuff going on. Nights on the street, crazy people fighting over cardboard boxes . . .

I've had it worse than this.

Sunday, 12 February

Today feels like a Sunday. I don't know why. Every day's the same down here. Same air, same light, same routine. Nothing changes. But for some reason today feels different. It's got that Sunday emptiness to it. That post-Saturday night sourness. The smell of dried sick.

Last night, after the lights went out, Bird kept up his ranting for an hour or so, then he banged around in the kitchen for a bit, went to the bathroom, made some horrible noises, and then everything went quiet. I couldn't get to sleep. I just sat there staring at the dark, listening to Jenny sleeping. She was making funny little breathy sounds, the unsettled sounds of dreaming—*ka ka ka . . . nuh nuh . . . mmnoo . . .*

Sometime in the early hours I heard a door opening and unsteady footsteps shuffling along the corridor. Someone knocked on a door. Then I heard a drunken whisper. I couldn't hear the words, but they didn't sound very nice. After a minute I heard Anja's voice hissing in reply.

"Go *away*."

Mumbling.

"No, *NO*! Just leave me *ALONE!*"

More mumbling, a drunken curse, then footsteps stumbled

back along the corridor, a door opened and closed, and it was quiet again.

Nothing happened the rest of the day. Nothing at all.

Tuesday, 14 February

I haven't written anything for a while. No reason, really. I had a few things I needed to think about. I wanted to empty my mind. Sort things out. I just wanted to be on my own.

You haven't missed much.

The drink and drugs have all gone. The cigarettes have all been smoked. The party's over, and now we're all paying the price. Fred's gone back to howling and moaning all day, and Anja and Bird are hungover and irritable. The place is a mess. No one's done any cleaning. The bathroom stinks. The schedule's been forgotten. No one cares any more. The evening meetings don't happen. We don't talk about escaping. We don't talk about anything.

I've been watching the clock. I've been sitting down at the dining table with my hands resting on my knees, keeping my eyes on the clock, watching the second hand, tapping a finger in time to the seconds. One, two, three, four, five, six . . . I just keep tapping, looking at the clock, looking away, tapping, tapping, counting the time in my head . . . one, two, three, four, five, six . . . until I get it right. What you have to do is count quite slowly and add the word *thousand* to every second. One, thousand . . . two, thousand . . . three, thousand. If you practise long enough you can measure the time pretty accurately.

For the last few days I've been counting the seconds, mentally keeping track of the minutes and hours. I've been checking *my* time against the *clock* time.

That's how I know He's messing with the time.

It's quite subtle. He slows it down or speeds it up very gradually. For example, on Monday afternoon I started timing things at two o'clock. By four o'clock *my* time, the clock on the wall said 3:45. OK, no big deal. I could have been wrong. But three hours later, three of *my* hours later, when it should have been 6:45, the clock said 5:55. And there's no way I'd miscalculated by that much. The clock on the wall was definitely slowing down. And as the evening passed, it got slower and slower.

Midnight came two hours late.

I carried on counting throughout the night.

Now *that* was really hard. I kept getting sleepy, disorientated, number blind. I kept losing it. But in the end I'm sure I kept a fairly accurate count. And I'm sure that the morning came two hours early.

It did.

I know it did.

I felt really pleased with myself for a while, like I'd caught Him out. I'd sat down and used my head and worked out what He was doing. I'd put one over on Him. Ha! Good for me. Linus the genius. The Greatest Thinker in the World. But then I thought—*Yeah, so you found out what's He's doing. So what? It doesn't change anything, does it? It doesn't get you anywhere. I mean, what are you going to do about it?*

I thought about that for a while, but I didn't get very far, so I went to see Russell and told him all about it.

"Are you sure?" he said.

"Positive. Sometimes He speeds it up and other times He slows it down. There's no set pattern. He does it at different times and at different rates, but He's definitely doing it."

"Well, well . . ." Russell said.

His face is getting thinner by the day. His skull seems to have shrunk, the skin sucked in like a dried-up balloon. The only part of him that isn't shrinking is his teeth.

He looked at me. "What do you think it means?"

"I don't know. That's why I'm asking you."

He smiled. "I thought you said you'd read my book."

"I have."

"Do you remember the chapter about time?"

"Yeah. Well, sort of. It was a bit hard to understand."

He nodded thoughtfully. "Early on in the chapter I mention a man called St Augustine. Ring any bells?"

"No," I admitted.

"Augustine of Hippo. He was a North African philosopher and theologian, one of the world's most influential thinkers on the nature of time. Many centuries ago he was asked the question, 'What *is* time?' And his reply was, 'If no one asks me, I know; but if any person should require me to tell him, I cannot.'"

Silence.

I looked at Russell, expecting him to go on, but he just sat there staring at the floor. I didn't know if he was deep in thought, falling asleep, or waiting for me to say something. I hoped he wasn't waiting for me to say something, because I didn't have anything to say. What was there to say? I mean, some old African guy tricks his way out of answering a difficult question . . . so what?

Anyway, I gave it a few moments, then said, "Right . . . I see."

Russell raised his head. "Doesn't help much, does it?"

"Not really."

"Look," he said, "all you have to remember is that time doesn't pre-exist. It's a manufactured quantity." He paused, breathing deeply, as if the act of speaking had tired him out. "The clock on the wall is nothing. It relates to nothing. It's just a machine . . . "

His voice trailed off and he put his hand to his head.

"Are you all right?" I asked him. "What's the matter?"

"Nothing."

"It's not nothing."

"Really—"

"No, not *really*," I said. "You're sick. You've been getting worse ever since you got here. Why don't you tell me about it? I might be able to help."

"I don't think so."

"How do you know? I might have secret healing powers." I don't know why I said that. It was meant to be a joke, I suppose. But it wasn't funny. It was an ultra-moronic thing to say.

He forced a smile to his face. "Can you keep a secret?"

I nodded.

"I don't want the others to know. Promise?"

"Yeah, I promise."

He took a deep breath, then sighed. "It's not what you think," he said. "I don't have AIDS. Not that it would matter if I did, of course. Well, it would . . . but I think you know what I mean."

I didn't, but I nodded anyway.

"It's a brain tumour," he said simply. "A primary brain tumour. Grade-four astrocytoma. I get very bad headaches . . . "

I didn't know what to say.

I said, "Oh."

Russell just looked at me.

"What's going to happen?" I said.

"Well, the position of the tumour..." He put his hand to his head. "It's here, deep within the brain. Surgery is too hazardous. The risk of damage is too high."

"What kind of damage?"

"Major damage. Partial paralysis, loss of speech..."

I'm not sure what happened to me then. I went a bit funny. As Russell carried on talking to me, telling me all about his tumour, my mind began to shift. I felt weirdly out of place, awkward and uncomfortable, too close, too far away, too young...

I can still feel it now.

I'm listening to him, but in a strange, disconnected kind of way. You know, when you're listening to somebody and your mind starts drifting away? I hear the words he's saying, but they're triggering the wrong things in my head. Like when he says *partial paralysis*. Just for a second I thought he said *Corporal* Paralysis—Major Damage, Corporal Paralysis—and in the same instant an image flashed into my mind, the cover of an old comic book. The comic was *Sergeant Fury*. Dad's favourite. He's got loads of old comics. He loves them. Collects them. War comics, superheroes, all the old Marvel comics. I used to read them all the time when I was a kid. I know them off by heart. I know all the covers. I can see them in my mind.

This time though, instead of seeing Sergeant Fury in my mind, gritting his teeth and heroically hurling a hand-grenade,

I see this decrepit old black man slumped against a bombed-out tank. His eyes are shocked white and his head is shrinking and a loose-helmeted medic is crouched down beside him, saying, "The position of the tumour... here, deep within the brain... surgery is too hazardous. The risk of damage is too high..."

"Linus?"

"Dad?"

"No, it's me. Russell. Are you all right?"

I looked up, my head suddenly clear again. "You've got cancer?"

"A brain tumour, yes."

"Is it curable?"

He shrugged. "With the best treatment possible I might have another year or so, maybe less. But down here, without medication, who knows? It could be a month, two weeks..."

The room fell silent. Our eyes met for a moment, and in that moment I knew he'd be dead very soon.

I said, "Is there anything I can do?"

He shook his head. "I need painkillers, steroids. I've asked for them, put them on the shopping list—"

"He won't give you anything."

"No."

"Is it getting worse?"

"Some days are better than others... some days..." His voice faded, and I thought for a moment he was dozing off again, but then he took a deep breath, straightened up, and smiled at me. "Hey, now," he said. "Don't look so glum. It's not as bad as all that. Just think of it as a change of timescale. That's what I do. You see, if you take a line, a world line, a lifeline if you like..."

He chatted away about different dimensions and relativity and stuff for a while, but I couldn't concentrate.

I was too depressed.

He's right though. About time. The clock on the wall *is* nothing. It's just a machine that makes three bits of metal go round in a circle. The Man Upstairs isn't messing with time, He's just messing with a machine. The only thing the clock affects is the accuracy of the dates in this diary. That's why I got mixed up when Bird arrived. I'd thought it was a Monday when he got here, but he said The Man had got him on his way home from work the day before, which I'd thought was a Sunday, which didn't make sense. But it probably wasn't a Monday after all. It was probably a Tuesday, or even a Wednesday.

God knows what's happened since then. How many days have I lost? Or gained? For all I know, today could be Wednesday, or Monday, or Thursday. But, like I said, what does it matter? Monday, Tuesday, Wednesday . . . they're only words, they don't have any real meaning. Down here is down here. A day is a day. The time is now. That's all there is to it.

Wednesday, 15 February

Things are beginning to get back to normal. Bird and Anja have got over their hangovers and got used to not smoking again. They're both still edgy and snappy all the time, but it's a controlled edginess now. It's not so spiky.

Fred's up and about again. He doesn't look too bad. A bit hollow-eyed, a bit twitchy, but that's about all. He seems to have got over the withdrawal symptoms a lot quicker than last time. I don't really know how heroin works or what it does to your body, but I guess it didn't take him so long this time because he hadn't been taking it that long.

The schedule's creaking back into operation too. The place is getting cleaner and it doesn't stink of cigarette smoke any more. We're still not talking very much, but at least everyone's sober and straight.

Normal.

Here's a normal day.

07:00: I wake up sweating. It's too hot. Sometimes He turns up the temperature at night. Other times He turns it down and I wake up shivering, but this morning it's too hot. I lie in bed thinking. Thinking of other times, when I was a little kid, when Dad was at home, when Mum was ...

Angry.

I always remember her angry. Angry or irritable. Or both.

I remember the garden too. The garden of the house we lived in before Dad got rich. The scrubby lawn, the hedge, the crumbling rockery, the fir trees . . . I can see it all, as clear as a bright-blue sky. At the far end of the garden there are two tall fir trees and a hedge of thick green privet. Wood pigeons call from the fir trees—hoo *hoo* hoo, hoo hoo . . . hoo *hoo* hoo, hoo hoo. I remember the hedge as a jungle. I remember summer. Slow-worms are resting in the sand and roots of the hedge. Slow-worms. Sleek brown tubes with skins of varnished leather. I sit cross-legged in the hedge-dirt watching them. They're not worms, they're not even snakes. I know that because I read my animal books. Slow-worms are legless lizards. They have hidden nubs of arm and leg bones to prove it. I sit in the dirt, scratching my arse, absently crumbling a clod of earth in my fingers, watching the slow-worms, and I remember Dad's joke.

Q: Why did the viper vipe 'er nose?
A: Because the adder 'ad 'er 'andkerchief.

I remember Dad's mouth, his smile, his straight white teeth. His bristly moustache. And I sit here in the dirt, rubbing the palm of my hand on my knee, singing a whispered song to myself (to the tune of "Three Blind Mice"): "*Hell-o Slow, hell-o Slow, what do you know, what do you know . . .* "—rocking back and forth like a praying mantis—" *. . . what do you know, Mis-ter Slow, what do you know, where do you . . . GO!*"

And on the word *GO!* I make a grab for one of the slow-worms, but I'm not quick enough.

I was never quick enough.

All I ever got was a handful of leaves and dirt.

08:00: the light comes on and my memories fade. I get out of bed and dress in my tattered clothes. Big T-shirt, padded shirt, hood, baggy pants, getting baggier by the day. Hi-Tec boots. I go to the bathroom, wash, clean my teeth, slip the sheet over my head and use the toilet. I walk back down the corridor, nod a silent greeting to Anja as she passes by the other way, and go into the kitchen. Make coffee. Sit down, wait for the lift to arrive.

08:45: Jenny comes in. We talk. She has a rash on her leg, tiny bites. I make a mental note to add lemons to today's shopping list. I seem to remember that lemon juice is good for flea bites.

08:55: Fred wanders in, shirtless, scratching his belly. He doesn't say much. He ruffles Jenny's hair. I tell him I want to see him later. He says OK, makes a cup of coffee, wanders back to his room.

09:00: the lift comes down. Food, juice, fruit, milk. Jenny helps me put it all away.

09:30: it's Bird's turn to make breakfast, but he forgets. Jenny makes toast. We eat together. I make some coffee and take it in to Russell. I want to talk to him about something, but his head is bad, so I leave him alone and go back to the kitchen.

The rest of the day drags on. The clock is set on slow. I talk to Fred, check on Russell, help Jenny with the cleaning. I lie down and think some more about the garden. I remember my clothes, my pale-blue shorts, my brown striped T-shirt, my sandals. I remember clutching a bamboo cane and a bottle of orange squash in my dirty hands, and I remember my daydreams. My imaginations. The garden is Africa, America, a desert plain of uncut grass, with rabbits' ears and ragged red roses. I remember plucking a rose thorn, licking it, and sticking it to my nose, making myself into a rhinoceros. Then, imagining rhinos and lions, I whip my bamboo cane at a big red ball, miss it, and the thorn falls off. I kick the ball and it sails up and over the rockery into a bed of red-hot pokers, flattening a full-bloomed stem. I glance quickly at the back door to check that Mum's not looking, then I scurry back up the garden to see if I can fix the broken flower. But I can't. So I snap it off and stuff it deep down into the base of the hedge. I know that Mum won't look in there, because she's scared of the slow-worms.

But what if she does?

And now my heart is hot with the memory of what happened early one summer when I stripped all the petals from Mum's pansies and she got really angry again.

"You little *sod*!"

Nasty eyes.

"What do you think you're *doing*? What's this?"

She's holding up a jam jar full of murky water. Bits of stick and pansy petals are suspended in the pale-brown goo. Insects too. And grass. Bugs. Leaves. Moss. Woodlice. Worms. Snails. A slug. Stones. Gravel. Mud.

What's this? A garden concoction, that's what it is.

What do you think you're doing? I'm collecting things in a water-filled jam jar and mixing them all up, just to see what happens. That's what I'm doing.

"What *is* it?" Mum snaps.

"Nothing."

"What do you think you're *doing*?"

"Nothing."

"Come here."

I can't move.

"Come *here*!" She shoves the jam jar into my hands. "Get rid of it. Go on . . . *now*!"

I start to cry. "Where?"

"Just get rid of it."

I take it up the garden path and start to empty it by the roses. "*Not THERE!*"

I see her standing in the doorway, a cigarette burning in her hand, and I don't know what to do. I'm scared.

"Just leave it," she spits. "Put it down." She draws hard on her cigarette. "*PUT IT DOWN!*"

I place the jam jar gently on the lawn, taking care not to spill it. The murky water rolls in the glass. I see bits of insects, beetle-wing boats, a black slug floating like a whale . . .

"Come here."

I shuffle down the path. My eyes are stinging. I need a wee. Mum grabs my arm and swings me round and slaps the back of my thigh.

"You little *shit*."

And again—*whack!*—really hard.

"Get upstairs."

I go up to my room and cry my heart out.

Sometime later she brings me biscuits and a glass of milk.

"Linus?" she says softly. "Linus?"

I can't speak. I'm trembling.

"It's all right now," she whispers. "Everything's all right. I won't tell Daddy. Daddy doesn't have to know . . ."

I don't know if any of this is true.

I can't sleep. I'm trembling.

Friday, 17 February

Yesterday I tried to escape.

It didn't work, and now we're all suffering for it.

Before I tried it, I wrote down what I planned to do in a page of my notebook and showed it to the others. Jenny thought it was a good idea. Bird and Anja thought it was a waste of time. Russell thought it was too risky. Fred didn't seem to think much of it either, but at least he was willing to give it a go. And eventually he persuaded the others to give it a go too. He can be very persuasive when he wants to.

So yesterday evening, about half an hour before the lift was due to go up, we got started.

While Jenny and Fred were in the kitchen, cooking up some bacon, I took a roll of bin liners down to the bathroom and began filling one with whatever rubbish I could find. At a prearranged signal, Jenny "accidentally' knocked over the frying pan, spilling bacon fat on to the cooker, and screamed *Fire!* Then she ran back to her room. As the flames spread on the cooker, Bird and Anja came running out of their rooms, shouting at the tops of their voices. Meanwhile, Fred had broken a leg off one of the dining-table chairs, dipped the end in the burning bacon fat, and set light to it. He quickly wrapped his head in a sheet, got up on the table and started poking the burning table leg at the grille in the ceiling.

While all this was going on I stayed in the bathroom, and as soon as all the shouting started I got to work. I had to move fast.

1) empty the rubbish out of the bin liner.

2) tear off five more bags from the roll.

3) quickly start stuffing one bag into another, then another, then another...

4) until I'd made a super-strong bin bag (six liners thick).

They were the extra-large bin liners, the ones you use for garden refuse. We hadn't specifically asked for them, and I don't know why He'd sent them down. I don't suppose He thought it mattered. Or maybe He did, thinking about it now. Maybe He knew what He was doing all along. Anyway, they were the extra-large bin liners, and I'm pretty small for my age, so when I climbed inside the super-strong bin liner, crouched down low, and scrunched myself up as tightly as possible, there was still enough room to fold the bin liner over my head.

And then I just waited.

Hoping.

Wondering...

I could hear all the racket going on outside—Fred cursing, Anja and Bird shouting—and then all at once that horrible piercing whistle started screaming out again. Not for long, but long enough to hurt.

And then suddenly it was quiet again.

I waited in the black plastic darkness.

Hoping, wondering...

Had He seen me making the bag?

Had He seen me getting into it?

Had the diversion worked?

Had I made the super-strong bin bag strong enough?

I waited.

Keeping perfectly still.

After a while I heard Fred's footsteps coming along the corridor. The bathroom door opened, his footsteps came closer, then the bin bag opened and he tipped some rubbish over my head. Not much, just enough to cover me. The bag closed. I felt him grip the bag and lift, and I held my breath, half-expecting the bag to split open, but it didn't. And then I was being carried along the corridor.

Like I said, I'm not that big, and I don't weigh very much at the best of times, but it was still a pretty remarkable feat. Fred had to carry me as if I weighed nothing, as if I was just a bag full of rubbish. Incredible. It was a very strange feeling, being carried along like a bag full of rubbish, and at one point I almost started laughing. I imagined myself as a tiny little man being carried home in a bag of shopping by an unsuspecting shopper, and when the shopper got home and started unpacking the bags, I'd jump out and scare them to death.

Doesn't sound very funny, does it?

You had to be there, I suppose.

I could feel Fred turning left now, heading along the little corridor towards the lift. And then, as gently as possible, but without making it too obvious that he was being gentle, Fred dropped me down inside the lift and left me there. Just another bag of rubbish.

All I had to do now was wait until nine o'clock and hope that 1) the lift went up as usual, 2) The Man Upstairs hadn't seen me getting into the bin liner, and 3) He hadn't been watching too carefully as Fred carried me along the corridor.

It was quite a lot to hope for.

Time passed slowly.

I waited.

Not moving.

Trying not to breathe too hard.

Then, after a few minutes, the lift door closed.

Tkk-kshhh-mmm . . .

I held my breath again.

The lift lurched and started going up.

Nnnnnnnn . . .

I couldn't believe it.

I was moving, I was going up, out of the bunker.

The lift stopped.

G-dung, g-dunk.

Everything was quiet.

I waited.

Nothing.

The door stayed closed.

I waited.

Nothing.

Then I heard a very faint hiss. A gassy sound. And a few moments later I smelled it. A chemical smell, not unpleasant. Like a hospital smell. Clean and gassy and . . .

"Oh, shit," I muttered.

And that was it.

I don't remember anything else.

Just senselessness.

When I woke up I was lying on my bed, back in my room, with a throbbing head and gummy eyes and a terrible ache in my stomach. I was shivering violently. It was freezing cold. My eyes felt as if they were glued together and there was a nasty sour taste in the back of my throat. I sat up, groaned, and cracked open my eyes.

Russell was sitting in the chair across the room.

"How are you?" he asked.

"Uh . . . ?"

"How do you feel?"

"Like shit," I said, rubbing goo from my eyes. "What happened?"

He gassed us all, that's what happened. Me in the lift, the others in the bunker. They were unconscious for about three hours. I was out for nearly twelve. He sent me back down in the lift. When the others came round they got me out and put me to bed.

"You didn't look too good for a while," Russell said. "We were all quite worried about you. Especially Jenny."

"Is she OK?"

"As well as can be expected."

"Good." I shivered. "Why's it so cold?"

"He's turned the heating off."

"Punishment, I suppose?"

Russell nodded. "That's not all, I'm afraid. While we were all unconscious, He came down and removed all the food and drink from the kitchen. All we've got left is water."

I opened my mouth to speak, but all that came out was a hacking cough that turned me inside out.

It's late now. I'm not feeling too bad. Not physically, anyway. I went in to see Jenny a while ago. She cried when she saw me. She said she thought I was dying.

"I'm not going to die," I told her. "I'm as tough as old boots."

"No you're not," she said. "You're weedy, like me."

I smiled. "I'm not *weedy*."

She wiped her nose. "You are."

"Yeah, well . . . us weedies are stronger than we look, aren't we? We have Weedy Power."

She grinned. "Weedy Power? What's that?"

"It's the stuff the others don't have. The stuff that keeps us going. Me and you, the Super Weeds."

"Yeah."

I didn't know what I was talking about. It felt all right though. It still feels all right. And as I sit here in bed writing these thoughts, I feel something I haven't felt in a long time, maybe never. I feel a closeness. It's a huge and overwhelming feeling that cancels out everything else, and I don't know what to do with it. It's so good it's beyond good, but at the same time it's unbearable. It fills me with visions of blackness and pain.

I can't say any more.

Sunday, 19 February

No food for two days now. Everyone's getting tired and irritable. No one has actually said they blame me, but I can see it in their eyes. We *told* you it was a stupid idea, we *told* you.

Yesterday the punishment continued with three hours of deafening noise. I don't know what it was. Some kind of abominable music—thunderous drums, horrible screeching sounds, wailing voices ... God, it was awful. And so *unbelievably* loud. There was nothing we could do. We all just lay down on our beds with sheets and clothing wrapped round our heads, our hands clamped tightly to our ears ... for three infernal hours.

Indescribable.

When it finally stopped, the silence shrieked with pain.

Monday, 20 February

Four hours of sweltering heat followed by four hours of arctic chill. Then the heat again, then the cold, the heat, the cold . . .

More skull-bursting noise.

Still nothing to eat.

All you can do is live it.

Live through it. Retreat inside your head, try to switch off, and wait it out.

Nothing lasts for ever.

You can take it.

Take it.

Take it.

Tuesday, 21 February

At last.

The temperature's back to normal and we've got food again. *Food.* Tons of it. When the lift came down this morning it was piled high with all kinds of stuff. Meat, bread, vegetables, fruit, chocolate . . . I've never seen anything so delicious in my life.

Foooooood!

Russell advised us to eat sparingly at first. He said if we ate too much on an empty stomach we'd get cramps. We all listened to him, nodding our heads and drooling, and then we all just piled in and gorged ourselves like starving animals. It was like one of those Roman banquets you see in films—bits of fruit and meat flying all over the place, everyone chomping and chewing and munching and dribbling and burping . . .

God, it felt good.

Now I'm lying on my bed drinking tea and grinning at the pain in my belly. It's a good pain. Good and full. Just to make it feel even better, I'm trying to remember how it felt to be hungry. It's impossible though. I know it felt bad, but I can't seem to dredge up the actual feeling of it . . .

Hold on.

Maybe Russell was right about the cramps.

I'm starting to feel something . . .

Like
No, it's not cramps
Something else
it's coming up all over all through
like electric like a
warm away gone away
warm and weightless
I think it's

perfect.

hot and thirstless I've never needed anything. Nothing is wrong. The walls are framed in tattered gold.

the garden the garden you're back in the garden again. never went away. yesyes, here you are, whupping your bamboo cane at the hedge and shaking the summer tears from your head. forget it. forget what? just do what you want. go down to the washing-line pole, go down, go round. go round and round the washing-line pole, round and round and round and round see it all against the whirling sky see it all the window house the roof the sun the pigeon trees the sky the fence the pyramid sky the window house where tigers wait the roof the sun the pigeon trees hoo hoo just look at the sunborn sky the hedge the rose of thorns rhinoceros horns the whirling sky where blackbirds soar the window house the roof of sun the big green trees the fence the gate the whirling sky
now we're clear.
doing this.
counting the animals in your animal book.

count the animals.

how many animals? count your fingers.

slowworm of course, he's in the book. slowworm rhinoceros tiger lion slug fox bear pigeon dog bear. no. rhinoceros tiger lion slug fox bear pigeon dog. is a slug an animal? slugdogslog. glug. a slug's a whale in a jam jar. hee. elephant whale insect mouse. what's that funny thing? weasel cow badger fox. no. flop-eared rabbit weasel.

daddy's joke

how do you know. no. what's the difference between a weasel and a stoat?

a weasel's weasily recognized and a stoat is stoatally different.

daddy tells rhymes.

> *budgies are bigger than grizzly bears*
> *and crabs are covered in fleas*
> *and parrots eat people and tigers eat pears*
> *and bees make honey from cheese.*

and the other one, the one with the buffaloes. round and round and round and round

> *buffaloes are hard to please*
> *they don't like mice and they don't like peas*
> *they only like to eat big things*
> *like mountain lions and eagles wings*
> *but bumble bees on the other hand*
> *eat tiny things like ants and sand*

and and and

and a million bee meals are so small
a baby buffalo could eat them all

and the one with the zebra. no. can't remember. so. fingers.
slowwormrhino nocerous tigerlion slugdog foxbear pigeondog
elephantwhaleinsectmouse weasel cowbadgerfox rabbit stoat
budgiegar fleacrab parrotpeople beebuffalobear eagullee
roundandroundandroundandround drink your orange, plastic
warm in the august sun. the washing-line pole is cold as lead.
good for swinging on. round and round. the rope line sways
to a rhythm. tink of tin knot collar tink of tin knot collartink
of tinknot collar
  how many animals? including people?
  we're all animals
  how many animals?
  27?
  enough for now.
  slowworm = 28.
  zebra = 29.
  2 foxies = 28.
  STOP
  this is where you are.
  here
  here sitting on the green grass in the whirling garden chewing
on a stick. drained and dazed. staring at the wall.
  there's only me.
  me you me
  I'm still here, Mister.
  The sun still moves in the sky.
  It doesn't matter what time it is.

A day lasts for ever. Let's go.

the garden path leads up to the rockery mountains where the stones are waiting for you to set light to a petrolsoaked spiderman with a banger in his spidershirt or to take him to the badlands where spiders hunch in web-hung caves their bulbous backs crossed like donkeys gripped tight in 8 black feet. donkeys and mexicans german soldiers sergeant fury maybe a mouse. a grizzly bear rroooaahh! or billy the kid. billy the magic man trapped in a cave with a donkeyspider. the spider spins him up in his silk and hangs him on a hook and billy waves his magic wand and taps his magic book and says i am not afraid to die like a man but the burning fuse of the banger melts his pretty face and when it blows it blows a hole in his plastic heart aaaahhhh!!! see all these small places are made for cowboys and indians to wait in ambush or to fight or to fall to their deaths or covered in honeyjam wait for the ants to come and all these small places are known unto you. so hongkong robocop gets it in the neck aaaahhhh!!!! these stones aren't fixed. the middle and bottom ones are set but the top ones wobble and lift when no one's looking like now. you can raise the roof on the sky of another world and let there be light. in flattened mud the colour of chocolate understone animals panic in the sun. woodlice scatter. worms wriggle and squirm. muscle-red yellow white like milksick. centipedes. a coughed-up slug. the hard brown coil of a millipede poke it with a stick. a long thin beetle specked with green skittles to a hole where it bows its head and ticks to the right then shudders and turns and ticks to the left going back in time. adjust your grip on the rock and look closer. see the slickness of the mud and the run of mystery trails. the beetle hole is rimmed inside with a pale white glow of tiny eggs. not quite white they have the colour of underground or dead things and you know you know that if you put them in an empty matchbox to see what happens they'll shrivel up to nothing. you know it. and now you hear your mother's voice.

LINUS!

a long way away

WHERE ARE YOU?

"I'm here."

Later. A million years later.

My head hurts. I feel sick.

The food was drugged.

He drugged the food.

I don't know what He put in it, something weird. Christ, I've never felt so weird in my life. Not bad-weird exactly. But not good-weird either. Just weird-weird. Different-planet weird. It was like I was someone else for a while. Somewhere and something else.

I can't think about it now.

I have to sleep.

OK, we've had a meeting. We had to get together again. We're all losing it. We need to recuperate, to console and comfort ourselves. Shit, we need *something*.

Looking round the table, all I could see were dying faces.

Jenny, poor kid. She can hardly speak. She sicked up most of the drugged food so she didn't suffer too much, but she's suffered enough. Sick people, bad dreams, the noise, the heat, the cold—she can't deal with all that. She's just a kid, for Christ's sake. It's too much.

I wrote a note this morning. I got a sheet of paper from the leaflet-holder on the wall and wrote: *Why don't you let Jenny go? Please? Just this one thing. Let her go. I'll pay for it, if that's what you want. I'll do anything. Tell me what you want me to do, and I'll do it. Just let her go. Please.*

I knew it was pointless.

A waste of time.

But I did it anyway.

Anja's just about had it. She's starting to look like one of those crazy women you see on the street, the ones who carry all their belongings in plastic bags and shout at cars. Her face is empty and mad.

Bird keeps staring at everybody like he wants to kill them.

Russell's getting sicker by the day. He can't speak properly. His speech is slurred and his face is dulled with pain.

Fred though . . . Fred still looks pretty strong. Hard and scary. Stony. I suppose he's used to it. Pain is nothing to him. It bounces off his head like raindrops off a rock.

And me? Well, I only know my face from the inside. It feels skinny and hard and raw with hurt.

So there we all were, six dying faces sitting round the table waiting for someone to speak. The silence was driving me mad.

"Come on," I said eventually. "We've got to do something. We can't go on like this. It's killing us."

Bird laughed. "Yeah, right. Good idea. *Do* something."

"Linus is right," mumbled Anja.

Bird gave her a cold stare. "You think so?"

Anja lowered her eyes.

Bird shook his head. "The last time we tried *doing* something it didn't work out too well, did it?" He looked at me. "If we hadn't *done* anything then, we wouldn't be suffering now."

"What do you want me to do?" I said. "You want me to apologize? OK, I apologize. I'm *sorry* I tried to get us out of here. Please forgive me."

Bird rolled his eyes.

I really hate that bastard. It's not just him, although he's bad enough, it's everything he represents. Commuter man. Suit man. Business man. Always moaning and whingeing about something, never satisfied. The train's late, it's too cold, I'm so *tired*. They're all the same, like full-grown babies in suits. Toys in their briefcases, trains instead of bikes, wives instead of mothers, beer instead of milk . . . you know what I mean? It's like they've grown up into nothing more than twisted children. They've taken their childhood, taken all the nice stuff, and turned it into crap. It really annoys me. I don't know why, it just does. People like Bird, I see them every day . . . I *used* to see them every day, when I was busking around the station. I used to see the way they looked at me, like I was nothing, a piece of shit. And I used to think—I could *buy* you. I could buy everything you own forty times over, so don't look at me like that.

And I think that's what sickened me the most. I hated the way they turned me into one of them.

Back to the table.

So Bird's rolling his eyes at me, giving me that piece-of-shit look, and it's really starting to annoy me. I'm about to say something to him when Jenny tugs at my hand and whispers something in my ear.

"What?" I say.

"Tell Him you're sorry," she whispers.

"I just did—"

"No, not Bird." She glances upwards. "Him, The Man Upstairs."

I look at her. "Sorry?"

"That's what He wants."

Bird leans across the table. "What's she saying?"

I ignore him. I can't stop smiling at Jenny.

"Hey," says Bird, slapping his hand on the table. I glare at him. His face is ugly and red. He says, "You yapping to your girlfriend or talking to me?"

I lean across the table and punch him in the head.

Meeting adjourned.

I've done what Jenny suggested. I've apologized to The Man Upstairs. I wrote another note. It wasn't hard. It's easy to say sorry, especially when you don't mean it. *Please forgive me for trying to escape*, I wrote. *I promise I won't do it again and I'm sorry for all the trouble I've caused. I realize it was a selfish thing to do. I'm genuinely sorry. Please don't punish us any more. Linus.*

I put the note with a shopping list and placed it in the lift.

I felt like a little kid sending a note to Santa. He doesn't believe in Santa, this little kid, but what harm can it do? What's he got to lose?

Note to The Man Upstairs: if you *are* reading this, please ignore the bit about not meaning it when I said I was sorry. I *am* sorry. Really. I was only pretending when I said I didn't mean it. I was just showing off. You know, trying to act tough.

OK?

Of course, if you're *not* reading this . . .

Thursday, 23 February

I've spent the whole day wallowing in self-pity. I don't know what's brought it on all of a sudden. Nothing terrible has happened, nothing out of the ordinary. I just woke up feeling really shitty. Don't get me wrong, I'm not complaining. In fact, I quite like feeling sorry for myself. It's got a warm, kind of snuggly feel to it. And it's not a bad thing to feel, is it? I don't think it is. As long as you keep it to yourself, I think self-pity is fine.

Of course, strictly speaking, I'm not keeping it to myself. I'm telling you about it. But if I accept you as me for the moment, then I think I can just about get away with it.

And if I can't?

Who cares?

The funny thing is, the more I feel sorry for myself, the less deadly it all becomes. Yes, it's crap. It's unfair. It's unbelievable. Unbearable . . . well, no, it's not unbearable. Nothing's un*bear*able. Unbearable means unendurable. If you can't endure something, you're dead. If it doesn't kill you, you've endured it. Isn't that right? It can't be unbearable. As long as I'm alive, I'm bearing it. And even if it *does* kill me, what will I care? I'll be dead. There'll be nothing to endure. Unless, of course, there really *is* a place called Hell.

Now there's a scary thought.

Eternal fire and damnation, devils, pitchforks, hot coals . . . Jesus, imagine *that*! You spend all your life laughing at the idea of Heaven and Hell, and then you die, thinking that's the end of it, but it's not. There really *is* a Hell. It's true, after all. It's *true*. And you're there, getting all burned up and cursed by the Devil, getting your eyes poked out by screaming goblins . . .

How annoying would *that* be?

There's another way of looking at it.

Let me think a minute.

Right.

Actually, this isn't anything to do with Hell. It was something else I was thinking about. I was thinking how unfortunate I am. How unfortunate to be plucked from nowhere and stuck in this shit-hole with no prospect of ever getting out. I was thinking—I must be one of the most unfortunate people in the world. And then I *really* started thinking about it.

OK, I told myself, forget about the others, just pretend you're on your own down here. It's just you. And then ask yourself, Am I the most unfortunate person in the world?

Think about it.

Theoretically, it must be possible to make a list. You start with the luckiest person in the world, the person who has everything they could ever want and more, then you work your way down through all the seven billion or so people who live on this planet until eventually you get to the most unfortunate person in the world. The unluckiest, the unhappiest, the one whose life is worse than everyone else's.

But then you've got a problem.

You've got this person, the most unfortunate person in the world, the person who's right at the bottom of the list, OK?

But just above this person, you've got the *second* most unfortunate person in the world. Now think about it. Which one would you rather be? The most unfortunate person in the world? Or the second most unfortunate person in the world? I know which one I'd choose. I'd go for the first one, The Most Unfortunate Person in the World. At least I'd *be* something. I'd have a title. I'd have something that no one else had. I mean, who the hell would want to be The *Second* Most Unfortunate Person in the World? Second is nowhere. Second is nothing. No one wants to know about second. And there's the problem. Because if being The Most Unfortunate Person in the World gives you something that the Second Most Unfortunate Person in the World doesn't have, then you can't be The Most Unfortunate Person in the World, can you? But then, if the Most Unfortunate title really belongs to the Second Most Unfortunate Person, that means *they've* got something the new Second Most Unfortunate Person doesn't have...

And on and on and on.

I can't remember what I was thinking about now.

It doesn't matter.

Whatever it was, it's made me feel better.

When the lift came down this morning there were two bags of food on the floor. We were all pretty hungry but we had no way of telling if it was drugged or not.

"I'm not touching it," Bird said. "I'd rather starve than go through all that again."

I looked at him. He glared back at me for a moment, then looked away. There's an ugly red welt on his cheek from where I hit him. I wish I hadn't hit him. I don't regret it, but I regret all the crap that comes with it—the friction, the inference, the possibilities, the reaction . . . the bruised knuckles.

I should have remembered Pretty Bob's advice.

Bob's a born fighter. He told me once that fighting is all about attitude. Hit early, hit hard, fight dirty. Cheat. And the thing I really should have remembered—if you're going to hit someone in the head, don't use your hands. Hands are fragile. They break. If you're going to hit someone in the head, use a stick, or a brick, or a guitar, or your head. Heads are hard and heavy. They hurt people. They surprise people. People expect a punch, they don't expect a head butt.

I hadn't used my head.

"Someone's got to try the food," I said. "We can't just stand here staring at it all day."

Jenny said, "Why don't we draw lots?"

"What for?" said Bird.

"To see which one of us is going to taste it."

"Not me," Bird snorted.

"Chrissake," said Fred, stepping forward and reaching into one of the bags. He pulled out an apple and sank his teeth into it. Half the apple disappeared in one bite. We stood there watching him. He chewed noisily for a while, swallowed, then ate the rest, core and pips and all. Without pausing, he reached into the bag again and selected a packet of cheese. Ripped it open, tore off a chunk, and stuffed it in his mouth.

"Hey," said Bird. "Slow down."

"You want some?" Fred said, offering the cheese.

Bird backed away. "Just take it easy. Leave some for the rest of us."

Fred grinned. "He who dares . . ."

"Don't eat it all," I said.

Fred stopped chewing and stared at me. "You what?"

I looked him in the eye. "Don't eat it all. Save some for Jenny. She needs it more than you."

He carried on staring at me for a long moment, his eyes hard and vicious, and I thought for a moment that he was going to crush my head or something. But after a while he just nodded his head, winked at Jenny, and gave me a cheesy smile.

"No sweat," he said. He dropped the cheese into the bag and picked out some chocolate and a loaf of bread. "Give me fifteen minutes with these. That should be enough. If I'm not lying on my back jabbering at the moon in fifteen minutes, then get stuck in, OK?"

"Thanks."

He stuffed a chunk of chocolate into his mouth and started off towards his room, keeping his eyes fixed on me as he went. He was still smiling, but it was the kind of smile that shrivels your heart. As he passed me he leaned down and spoke quietly in my ear. Two short words. "Watch it." And then he was gone.

The food was fine. No drugs, no weirdness, just a nice full belly. It looks like Jenny was right. He just wanted me to say sorry.

It baffles me.

I've been lying here for the last two hours trying to work out if it means anything. I apologize, He gives us food. What's that all about? Does it mean He's got a weak spot? Is He a sucker for good manners? Or is He trying to *train* us? I don't think so. I don't think it means anything. I think He was probably going to feed us anyway. The food coming down this morning, the morning after I apologized, that was just a coincidence. He's just toying with us. Give and take. Good and bad. Hot and cold. The food wasn't a gift or a reward or anything . . .

Or maybe it was.

Maybe that's His thing, punishment and reward. You know, like we're rats in a cage and we have to learn which buttons to push. Push the right one and we get some food, push the wrong one and we get whacked.

Maybe that's it.

I don't know.

I'm fed up thinking about it, to be honest.

I'm fed up thinking about anything.

And I'm fed up talking to you, as well. It's like talking to a brick wall. I mean, what do you do? Nothing. You just sit there saying nothing and doing nothing. You make me sick.

God, I want to *do* something. Anything. Dig a hole, smash down the wall, blow something up, hit someone, anything . . .

I just want to *DO SOMETHING*!

11:30 p.m.

Sorry.

Saturday, 25 February

Two days of food, two days of peace and quiet. Normally I like a bit of peace and quiet, but this isn't normal. Nothing's normal any more. This isn't a relaxing sort of peacefulness, it's dull and deadly, like everyone's given up hope.

We all spend a lot of time alone in our rooms now, me included. It's not healthy, I know, but it's hard to find the energy to do anything else. I do my best. I force myself to get up and walk around every couple of hours or so. It keeps me sane and stops my head imploding. Also, I'm still looking for a way out. My brain keeps telling me I'm wasting my time, but my heart hasn't given up yet.

Jenny joins me on my walks quite often, and sometimes Fred tags along for a while, but the rest of them rarely get out of bed any more. They only show their faces when the lift comes down or when they need to go to the toilet.

I don't know what they do in their rooms.

Anja cries a lot.

I went to see her yesterday. I don't know why I bothered. I knew it was pointless.

Knock, knock.

"What?"

"It's me, Linus."

"What do you want?"

"Nothing, really. I just wondered how you're doing."

"Go away."

Russell sleeps most of the time.

I don't know what Bird does. I never hear any noise from his room, and I very rarely see him. Even when I do, he doesn't speak to me. He still hasn't forgiven me for hitting him. Fair enough, I suppose. I expect he's planning some kind of humiliating retaliation. Good luck to him. It takes a lot to humiliate me.

Jenny sings when she's on her own. I hear her sometimes, singing quietly to herself—kids' songs, made-up songs, unthinking songs. It's a very nice sound, but very sad too.

And what about me? What do I do in my room?

I think.

I write.

I don't read the bible.

I laugh.

I shudder.

But most of the time, I just think.

A lot of it is escaping stuff, stuff I can't tell you about. Not yet anyway. Hopefully never. And the rest of it . . . I don't know. It's mostly too boring to talk about. Dad, Mum, memories, feelings . . .

Who wants to know about that kind of crap?

I'll tell you one thing though.

When I get out of here, the first thing I'm going to do is find myself a nice quiet room with a nice comfy settee and a nice big TV, and I'm just going to lie there and watch the most boring programmes I can find until every little thought has been sucked out of my head. Then I'm going to lie there some more until my emotions are drained, and then I'm going to eat a LARGE quarterpounder with cheese, with LARGE fries, and I'll wash it all down with a LARGE Coke with tons of ice, and then I'm going to have a steaming-hot bubble bath, and I'm not getting out until the water's cold and my fingers have gone all wrinkly.

Then I'm going to have another LARGE quarterpounder with cheese.

And then . . .

Well, I'll think about that when the time comes.

Right now, I'm going to sleep.

Tuesday, 28 February

Now I've really gone and done it. I tried to escape again. This time I didn't tell anyone else what I was doing.

This time . . .

Shit.

This time I think I've made a big mistake.

I thought I'd got it all worked out. I used my head. I used logic. I used past experience. What's the problem? I asked myself. Step back and strip it down to the basics, Linus. What. Is. The. Problem? Well, the problem is—He's up there and we're down here. And as long as He stays up there, we're staying down here.

Right?

Right.

So why not try to get Him down here?

He came down before, didn't he? He likes to punish you. If you do something wrong, He punishes you. The last time you tried to escape He gassed the lot of you, then came down here and took all the food away. Think about it. He came down in the lift. So He must have some kind of remote-control device, otherwise He wouldn't have been able to get back up again, would He?

So all you've got to do is get Him down here, and then do the necessary.

Just do it.

So I spent Saturday and Sunday thinking and planning, and by Monday I was ready. I had a plan. Admittedly, the plan was full of holes, but the way I saw it a plan full of holes was better than no plan at all.

Step 1: I got some bin liners from the kitchen, filled a saucepan with water, and pretended to clean up my room. Wetting a cloth, wiping down surfaces, careful not to wet the cloth too much.

Step 2: I stripped the sheet off my bed and took it into the bathroom. Filled the bath, put the sheet in the bath, gave it a wash. Then I took the sheet back to my room and hung it over the door to dry.

Step 3: I got the jitters. I re-realized how holey the plan was and I was struck with the absolute certainty that it wasn't going to work. Nothing is 100 percent certain, I told myself. Just ignore it.

Step 4: I left my room, went over to the dining table and picked up a chair. Then I went over to the clock on the wall and smashed it to pieces with the chair. I put the chair down and went back to my room.

Step 5: I waited. I sat down on my bed and stared at the grille in the ceiling. Read my thoughts, Mister, I thought. I broke your clock. Punish me. I broke your clock. If you want to carry on messing with the time, you're going to have to come down here and fix it. Did you hear what I said? I broke your clock. Come on, punish me. What's the matter? You scared? Come *on* . . .

Click.

The lights go out.

I hear voices outside.

"What's going on?"

"Shit, what now?"

"Hey!"

Then,

Knock, knock.

"Linus?"

It's Jenny.

"Go back to your room, Jen," I call out. "Just stay calm. It'll be all right."

"What's happening?"

"Nothing. Just go back to your room, get into bed, and lie still."

Then I hear the hissing sound. I look up at the grille. I can smell it, the smell of chemicals, growing stronger.

Step 6: I grab a bin liner from under my bed and rip a hole in it to make a collar. Pull the black plastic over my head and roll it tightly around my neck. Grab the damp sheet from the door. Tear off a strip, dip it in the water-filled saucepan, wind the strip round my mouth and nose. And now the chemical smell is getting stronger. The air is pungent, gassy, hard to breathe. Eyes stinging. I drape the damp sheet over my head, wrap it round, round and round, over my head, eyes, mouth, nose, tuck it into the bin-liner collar. Breathe easy. Pour water over my cloth-wrapped head. Get into bed. Pull up the blanket. Breathe easy. Concentrate...stay awake. Lie still...go limp...play dead.

The gas keeps coming.

Hissing in the dark.

How long?

One, thousand . . . two, thousand . . . three, thousand . . . four, thousand . . .

Count.

Concentrate.

Stay awake.

How long?

Minutes.

Getting heavy-eyed.

Count.

One, thousand . . .

Think.

Stay awake . . .

The hissing stops.

The lights come on.

I'm still alive.

I'm conscious.

Sick, dizzy, dopey . . . but conscious.

Now I just have to wait.

A minute.

Keep quiet.

Five minutes.

Lie still.

Ten minutes.

Listen.

Tkk-kshhh-mmm . . .

The lift door closing.

Nnnnnnnn . . .

Going up.

G-dung, g-dunk.

The lift stops.

Pause. A whirring.

Clunk . . . click . . . nnnnnnnn . . .

The lift coming back down.

Step 7: I grab the saucepan, empty it, get out of bed. I run. My legs are jelly, my head's all over the place. The air is foul, thick with gas. Quick, get to the lift, back against the wall, grip the saucepan. Stay awake. It's coming down . . . *nnnnnnn . . .* here it comes, here He comes . . . *g-dung, g-dunk . . .* get ready . . . the door's opening . . . *mmm-kshhh-tkk.*

Raise the saucepan, ready to strike.

Ready.

Ready . . .

Nothing happens.

Wait.

Come *on* . . .

Where are you?

Nothing.

Where *are* you?

I stood there for a long time. Back to the wall, saucepan raised, heart beating hard, hazy head wrapped in plastic and wet cloth, eyes streaming . . . and I knew He wasn't there.

He wasn't in the lift.

I'd failed. I knew it.

Eventually I had to face up to it.

I stepped away from the wall and looked inside the lift.

The only thing in there, positioned carefully in the middle of the floor, was a grubby £10 note folded into the shape of a butterfly. It was my £10 note. I don't know how I knew, I just knew. It was the £10 note I'd had in my sock when He got me. The one He'd taken from me a lifetime ago.

Now everything is really bad and it's all my fault. Everyone except Jenny and Russell hates my guts for putting them through another dose of the gas. Even Russell was a bit frosty for a while.

"You should have discussed it with me," he said.

"You would have told me not to do it."

"Perhaps."

"You would. I know you would. That's why I didn't tell you."

"Well, anyway, it's done now."

It's done, all right.

The food's stopped again. The heating's off. We don't even have a clock any more.

And that's not the worst of it.

It's not even *close* to the worst of it.

This morning something *really* terrible happened. He raised the punishment to another level. Even now, I can still hardly believe it.

I was lying in bed shivering, trying to work out what I felt worst about. The cold? The hunger? The emptiness in my head? The ache in my bladder? There wasn't much I could do about the first three, so I decided to act on the fourth. I got out of bed, wrapped the blanket round my shoulders and started for the bathroom. As I left my room I saw Bird standing over by the lift. He looked across at me, then quickly looked away, making a big show of ignoring me. I muttered something under my breath and wasted ten seconds or so staring moodily at his back. Then Fred loped down the corridor towards the kitchen and I turned my attention to him. Shirtless, pale, and tired. He nodded at me but didn't say anything. I waited for him to pass, and was just about to turn down the corridor when I heard the lift coming down. I paused. I knew it was going to be empty, foodless, but I still had to wait and see.

The lift is the thing.

The thing.

It's impossible to resist. You can't ignore it. It's like checking your pockets for cash when you know they're empty. You've already been through them twice, you know they're empty, but you still have to check them again, just in case.

Anyway, the lift came down.

The door opened.

It wasn't empty.

There was a dog in there.

I've seen some scary-looking dogs in my time, but this . . . God . . . this was something else. A Dobermann. One of those big ugly ones. Dark brown, nearly black. Long head, small pointy ears, powerful shoulders. Skinny, bony, half-starved. Burning eyes, bared teeth, snarling black lips.

We all froze. Bird, Fred, me, the dog. For about half a second, nothing happened. The dog just stood there, staring at us, tall, rigid and silent, and the three of us just stood there too, rooted to the spot, staring back at it. And then suddenly, without a sound, the dog shot out of the lift and launched itself at Bird. No growling, no barking, nothing—just a black streak and a flash of wicked teeth. It was breathtaking. Bird twisted away and threw his hands up to protect his throat, but the dog was on him like a guided missile. It jumped up and sank its teeth into his neck, just above the shoulder, and Bird screamed and fell to the floor with the dog on top of him.

I couldn't move. I was petrified. But Fred was already up and running. Before I knew what was happening he was halfway across the corridor, whipping the belt from his trousers as he ran, heading for Bird and the dog. Bird was sobbing now, a terrible, gut-wrenching sound. I could hear teeth on bone. The dog was gnawing on his neck. There was blood all over the place. Fred didn't hesitate for a second, he just ran up to Bird and the dog and looped his belt round the Dobermann's throat. He put his knee in the dog's back and pulled the belt tight, twisting it in his hands, then heaved, pulling upwards and back, tightening the belt as he pulled. The dog jerked up into the air, twisting and snapping like a crazy thing, and then Fred swung it round and hammered it down on the floor. Before the dog had a chance to get up again, Fred dropped down on top of it and grabbed its snout in one huge hand, clamping its mouth shut. He hooked his other arm under the dog's neck, then let go of the snout, locked his arms together, gritted his teeth, and squeezed. Tighter and tighter, pressing down on the dog's head, crushing its throat . . . choking, pressing, crushing. The dog struggled horribly, kicking its legs and flexing its body, but Fred had all his weight on it now. The dog couldn't move. Couldn't bite. Couldn't breathe. Fred squeezed harder, groaning and straining, forcing the dog's head down with all his strength, until eventually I heard a dull *snap*, and the beast went limp.

Fred didn't let go. He sat there for a minute or so, drenched in sweat, still gripping the dog's head, making absolutely sure it was dead. Then, with a final sigh, he let go. The lifeless

Dobermann slumped to the floor, its head flopping loosely on its broken neck. Fred looked at it for a moment, no expression in his eyes. Then he stood up, dragged the dead dog into the lift, and threw it dismissively into the corner.

The others had come out now. Jenny, Anja, Russell. They were standing huddled together at the end of the corridor, their eyes shocked with fear and disbelief. Jenny was crying and Anja was staring open-mouthed at Bird. Bird wasn't moving. He lay on the floor with his knees pulled up to his chest and his arms cradled over his head.

Russell shuffled over to him.

I crossed over to Fred.

"You all right?" I asked.

"Yeah," he said, panting. He wiped sweat from his face and glanced inside the lift. The dead Dobermann was splayed out on its side. Its ears were laid back and its mouth was hanging open, revealing two rows of blood-flecked yellow teeth.

"Shit," I said.

Fred laid his hand on my shoulder. "Never a dull moment, eh?"

Bird's not dead. He's hurt quite badly, but he's not dead. He's got a nasty gaping wound in his neck and he's lost a lot of blood. Russell cleaned the wound with water, then left it to bleed. Anja was all for bandaging it but Russell said it's best to let it bleed. It helps to clean the wound, apparently.

"Will he be all right?" I asked him.

Russell shrugged. "It's a nasty bite and it's near the head. But as long as it doesn't get infected, he should be OK."

"What happens if it does get infected?"

"Don't ask."

"Is there anything we can do?"

"He needs antibiotics."

"No chance. Anything else?"

Russell laughed humourlessly. "We could always try praying."

So that was Monday. Or Tuesday, or Wednesday...

That was today.

Now it's nearly midnight and everything is quiet. I'm hungry. I'm cold. I'm all mixed up. Was it my fault He sent down the dog? Am I to blame for Bird getting hurt? Or would it have happened anyway? I don't know. I really don't know. But whatever the answer is, I'm not going to feel bad about myself. I can't afford to. I *can't* blame myself. I mean, you do what you do, don't you? You just do it. What else can you do?

What would *you* do?

If you were me, what would you do? Give up? Would you just give up? Would you lie down and cry? Would you just lie down and take what's coming. Take what you're given. Take it...

Maybe I should?

Maybe I should just give up. Give in. Here, have my life. Go on, take it. Do what you want with it. I don't care.

I don't know.

Maybe I should try apologizing again, only this time add a bit more grovel to it. I could get down on my knees, close my eyes, tell Him how wonderful He is...

On second thoughts, I think I'd rather just give up.

Wednesday, 29 (?) February

Midday.

No food.

We're still putting a shopping list in the lift every night, but when the lift comes down in the morning the list has gone and there's no food, no nothing. Just an empty lift. There's still a few bits and pieces of food left in the fridge, so we're not starving yet. Just hungry and cold. The heat's still off and it's absolutely freezing down here. The walls are filmed with ice.

Bird's not looking too good. His neck's gone red and he's got a fever. He's spent the last two days lying in bed, moaning and groaning all the time. Mind you, that's what he does most of the time anyway, so I'm not too worried about it.

A disturbing moment. I came across Russell in the corridor this morning. He was just standing there staring at the wall.

"Mr. Lansing?" I said. "Russell?"

He turned and looked at me. "Hello there."

"What are you doing?"

He smiled. "Interview."

"What?"

"They want to see me about something." He winked. "Disciplinary procedure."

I didn't know what to say.

I left him there looking at the wall.

Jenny's got a bad cold. At least, I hope it's just a cold. Her eyes are all runny and she keeps coughing all the time.

Apart from all that though, everything is just fine.

Late evening.

Quiet. White. Cold. Dead.

I put a note in the lift tonight asking for antibiotics and something for Jenny's cold. I know it's a waste of time, but I can afford it. I've got all the time in the world. I mean, we might not have any food or heat in here, but the one thing He can't take away from us is time. He can mess around with our perception of it—or at least He could before I smashed up the clock—but He can't *deny* us time. We've got plenty of that.

Plenty of time.

I've been thinking about it.

Time . . .

Tick tock.

First thing. I've just realized what day it is, 29th February. I think it's the 29th anyway. I think this year is a leap year. I can never remember how you're supposed to work it out.

Not that it matters.

But if I'm right, I've been here a month. Actually, it's 32 days. I've just worked it out. 32 days. 768 hours. 46,080 minutes. 2,764,800 seconds. Give or take a day or two. Or three.

It's all relative, of course.

Say I've been here a month. I'm sixteen years and four months old (give or take a few days), which is 196 months. So a month to me is 1/196th of my life. But Russell . . . well, let's say he's seventy. Seventy years is 840 months. So he's been here for 1/840th of his life. And Jenny, in her terms, has been here longer than both of us. I don't know exactly how old she is (I know she's nine, but I don't when she's ten), but if we say for the sake of simplicity that she's ten, that means she's been here for almost 1/120th of her life.

See? A month means different things to different people. That's what I mean by time being relative.

Time . . .

Yeah, I've been thinking about it. I've thought about it so much, I've thought myself into a dead end.

And another thing . . .

It's hard.

Hold on.

Let me get this straight.

Right, it goes something like this. You've got the past, the present, and the future, OK? Time-wise, that's all you've got. Then, now, and when. The past has gone. You can't exist in the past, can you? It's gone. You can remember it, but you can't exist in it. And you can't exist in the future either, can you? It hasn't happened yet. So that leaves the present. Now. But if you think about it, if you ask yourself what the present actually is, *when* it is . . . I mean, how long is the present? How long is *now*? This moment, right now, the moment you exist in. How long does it last? A second? Half a second? A quarter of a second? An eighth of a second? You can go on halving it for ever, again and again and again. You can take it down to an infinitesimally small period of time, a squillionth of a nanosecond, and then you can *still* halve it again. How can you exist in such an immeasurably small period of time? You can't, can you? It's too small to experience. It's gone before you know it.

But if you can't exist now, and you can't exist in the future or the past—when the hell *do* you exist?

Time . . .

I went to see Russell about it. That's the kind of thing he knows about, time and stuff. But he was in a daze again. He thought I was someone called Fabian.

I don't suppose it matters.

Thursday, 1 March

We're completely out of food now. This morning we shared out the last of the crackers. Two each. Yum yum. There's nothing like a stale cracker to raise the spirits.

Bird's up and about. His neck and half his face have turned a weird shade of blue, and he's got these horrible purply-red blotches all over his skin. He's walking about though, so he can't be that bad. I asked him how he was feeling, but he wouldn't even look at me.

He tried to get an extra cracker. He said he was sick, he needed the extra energy. He wanted one of mine. Said it was my fault he was sick, so I should give him one of my crackers.

Fred told him to shut up.

It's funny. Bird hates Fred. I don't think he hates him as much as he hates me, but it's pretty close. He thinks Fred's an idiot. Coarse. Brutal. Scummy. He thinks he's a lowlife. But now he owes him his life, and he's not sure how to deal with it. He doesn't know how to show gratitude. If it was me, I'd just say thanks, thanks a lot for saving my life, and leave it at that. But Bird seems to think he owes Fred something more, like he's beholden to him or something. So he acts all subordinate, all cringey, but at the same time he can't hide his contempt for him. It creeps into his smile like a really bad smell.

It's pathetic really.

I had a long chat with Russell this evening. I didn't mention the incident when he went a bit funny, but I think he knows about it. He looked a bit embarrassed, like a drunk who knows he's done something stupid but can't remember what it was. Anyway, Russell told me all this stuff about when he was a kid, about his parents and school and what is was like growing up black and gay. He made it sound funny, but I think he had a pretty tough time. He got beaten up quite a lot.

When the kids at boarding school first started picking on me, I thought it had something to do with Dad being rich, that the other kids were just jealous, but I soon realized they had nothing to be jealous about. Their parents were all rolling in money too, *huge* amounts of money, and at least half of them had *real* celebrities for parents. Real A-list celebrities. Lords and ladies, minor royals, MPs, rock stars, film stars, that kind of thing. Compared to their parents, my dad was nothing. And then I started thinking that maybe that was why they picked on me. Because I was common, working class. I had no breeding. Or maybe they didn't like my long hair? The way I speak?

Or maybe they just didn't like me?

That's possible, isn't it? Maybe I'm not very nice? I mean, you can't tell, can you? You can't tell if you're nice or not. You think you are, but everyone thinks they're nice. Everyone thinks they're all right.

Anyway, it doesn't matter now. They picked on me, it doesn't matter why. They just did.

Russell asked me what I'm going to do when I get out of here, if I'm going back home to Dad.

"I don't know," I said. "Probably. The street's all right for a while, but in the end it's no better than anywhere else. Same crappy people, same crappy life. Same old shit. At least Dad doesn't steal my stuff."

"Do you miss him?" Russell said.

"I don't know him enough to miss him."

Russell looked at me.

I sighed. "Yeah, I miss him."

Dad tried to find me when I first ran away. He had all these posters printed up, you know, the usual MISSING PERSON kind of thing, with my name and photograph and everything. He had them stuck up all over the place. I saw quite a few around London, in railway and underground stations mostly, but Dad didn't actually know where I was, so he had the posters put up all over the country. I found out about it from this girl I met who'd come down from Northampton. Sophie. I met her one day hanging around outside McDonald's at Liverpool Street. She was dressed in a threadbare skirt, thin black tights, and bright-red monkey boots. She was kind of nice. Anyway, we got talking and she said she recognized me from posters she'd seen in Northampton.

After that I cut my hair short and dyed it blond.

Dad hired a private detective too. A dirty little man in a cheap suit. He started sniffing around, asking questions, showing people my photograph, but he didn't last long. Pretty Bob tracked him down and beat him up. I don't think he did it for my sake, he just likes beating people up.

See?

Same crappy people . . .

I've had enough of this.

Sunday, 4 March

Haven't managed to write for a while. Can't think of anything to say. I'm hungry, it's cold, I'm bored, scared, fed up.

The same old stuff.

God, I'm *so* fed up.

It gets to the point when you can't do anything. You can't think any more. You can't remember anything. You don't feel anything. You can't even get angry any more. You just lie on your bed all day staring into space. Then the lights go out and you stare at the darkness.

The lights come on.

The empty lift comes down.

The day passes.

The empty lift goes up.

The lights go off.

I try to keep thinking, but the more I concentrate, the more confusing it gets. What am I doing? Thinking. Thinking? What's that? *Thinking?* How does *that* work?

I think about that and my head starts spinning.

It gets worse.

I imagine myself as being nothing more than sixteen years of bone, skin, muscle, brain, blood, meat, and jelly. I imagine symbols inside my head. Electric things. Circuits. Tubes. Spatial patterns frozen in time. Tiny things. Bits of stuff. Short jaggedy strings. Carbon. Components.

Stuff.

I think about it.

I think about what that stuff can do.

It can move me. It can walk. It can breathe. It grows. It can see. It can hear, feel, smell, taste. It can like and hate. It can want. It needs. It can fear. It can speak. It can laugh. It can sleep. It can play. It can wonder. It can tell lies. It can remember. It can live with doubts and uncertainties. It can sing, la la. It can dance. It can dream. It bleeds. It coughs. It blinks. It shivers and sweats. It can live without love.

It's complicated.

It can:

Analyse.

Coordinate.

Destroy.

Dream.

Secrete.

Control.

Generate.

Degenerate.

Synthesize.

Emote.

Regulate.

Calculate.

Imagine.

It can run.

Play.

Jump.

Judge.
It can catch a ball.
And dance.
And fight.
And cry.
It can know at night that the morning will come.
It can spit.
Recognize.
Ride a bike.
It can kill.
Whistle.
Ask.
And forget.
It can hope.
And hurt.
It can come to know that there's nothing to know.
And it can, and it will, close my eyes.

Tuesday, 6 March

I'm feeling better now. We've still got no food, and it's still very cold, but I seem to have found some energy from somewhere, and I've managed to shake off the worst of the gloom.

I don't feel quite so desperate any more.

I'm not sure what happened to me over the last few days. I lost myself, I think. I sank down into a hole for a while.

They're tricky things, holes. You don't know you're in one until you get out.

This morning I killed and ate a couple of cockroaches. Big ones. They were in the kitchen, behind the burned-out cooker. I was just poking around down there, having a look. You never know what you're going to find down the back of a cooker, do you? The cockroaches were on the wall. I grabbed them fast, squished them up, stuck the goo in a cup, mixed in a bit of cooking oil, and swallowed the lot.

It tasted foul.

Later. 11:57 p.m. to be precise.

We've got a new clock.

A few hours ago the knock-out gas came on. I was in my room, sitting on the bed trying to get some knots out of my hair. I heard the hissing, looked up, and then I smelled the chemicals. I got up and started wrapping a sheet round my head, but it was too late. My eyes started streaming, the stuff got into my lungs, and that was that.

When I woke up I went out and checked on the others. They were all up and about, apart from Bird, who was lying on his bed gasping like a stranded fish. I haven't seen him for a while and I didn't realize how bad he's got. He looks terrible. His skin's all streaked and discoloured, his head's swollen, his neck's as stiff as a board, and his eyes are bulging like mad. It was a really shocking sight. Too much to cope with.

I left his room and went to join the others.

We had a good look round to see if He'd come down and done anything while we were all knocked out, but the only thing we could find was the clock. A brand-new clock.

Exactly the same as the old clock.

Just for a moment I had an irresistible urge to smash it.

That was about it.

We all hung around for a bit, trying to think of something to say, but no one could think of anything. New clock? Big deal. You can't eat it, can you? After a while the silence got too much and everyone started drifting back to their rooms.

I followed Russell and caught up with him at his door.

"Can I have a word with you?" I said.

He looked at me with distant eyes.

"About Bird," I said.

"Who?"

"Bird. I think he's really ill."

Russell just nodded.

I said, "Have you seen him recently?"

"Who?"

"*Bird.*"

Russell blinked. "I'm sorry, I'm very tired. Can we talk about this some other time?"

"But I think he's—"

"There's nothing you can do about it. He's dying. We're all dying. You might as well get used to it."

Then he turned and shut the door on me.

It's five minutes before lights-out. I wonder if they're going to be five long minutes or five short minutes. I wonder how He adjusts the time. Does He do it manually? Is it automated? Computerized? Has He got the clock linked up to some kind of time-adjusting mechanism, something He downloaded from the Internet or bought at one of those gadget places in Tottenham Court Road?

And another thing I wonder.

I wonder if He read my notebook when He came down here. Did you?

Hey, Mister, did you read this when you came down here? Did you take a peek at my innermost thoughts? Did you? No, I don't think you did. In fact, I *know* you didn't. You see, I'm pretty sneaky. I can tell if this notebook's been moved. I can tell if it's even been *touched*. You want to know how? Well, tough, I'm not telling you.

Mind you, I don't need to be *that* sneaky when it comes to you. I would have known anyway. If you'd touched this notebook I would have smelled it a mile away. The pages would have reeked of shit.

175

Thursday, 8 March

A word about Jenny.

We spend a lot of time together. Even in the bad times—when I'm feeling down, or she's feeling sick, or the other way round— we spend hours together every day. Sometimes we talk, sometimes we don't. It doesn't matter. Just being together is enough. I tell her stories, make up jokes. We play word games. Russell joins in sometimes, when he's not too tired. Fred occasionally. But mostly it's just me and Jenny. If I'm not in the mood for stories or jokes, she just babbles on about her friends, or her family, or what she thinks about things—pop groups, TV, dogs, clothes. I don't have to do anything. I just listen. Nod my head. Say uh-huh now and then. Or not. It doesn't matter.

It's good.

It keeps us both going.

Me more than her, probably.

She's coping pretty well. She *looks* a mess—skinny, dirty, tired—but then we all look a mess. The difference with Jenny is her eyes. Even when they're runny, her eyes are clear. Alive. As bright as the day she arrived. The rest of us have dead eyes.

Earlier this evening she told me that Anja has some food.

"*What?*" I said.

"Cornflakes. I saw them in her room."

"What were you doing in her room?"

Jenny looked a little embarrassed. "I wanted to ask her about something."

"What?"

She blushed. "Nothing . . . just a girl thing."

"Oh, right."

She smiled awkwardly. "I knocked on her door and went in. I didn't *mean* to be rude. I thought I'd heard her say, 'Come in.' But I don't think she did because when I went in she was putting a packet of cornflakes under her bed. I saw her, Linus. She shouted at me. Told me to get out."

"Cornflakes?"

She nodded. "I saw them."

"Are you sure?"

"I *saw* them."

I suppose she must have had them stored away since before the food ran out. So while the rest of us have been starving to death she's been munching away on cornflakes.

"Stay here," I told Jenny.

I went out into the corridor, stomped across to Anja's room and barged in without knocking. She was sitting on the floor with her back against the wall, dressed only in her underwear. White lace, all grubby and stained.

"Hey," she said. "What the fuck —?"

"Shut up."

I went over to her bed and looked underneath it. There was nothing there. I went over to the bedside cabinet and opened the door. Meanwhile Anja had got to her feet and was screaming at me.

"What the hell do you think you're *doing*? Get away from that. How *dare* you come in here without . . . *hey*!"

Inside the cabinet, as well as the cornflakes, there was a thick crust of mouldy bread, half a bar of chocolate, and a slab of dried-up cheese.

"Now, hold on a minute," Anja spluttered. "Listen, I can explain ..."

I swept the food into my arms, kicked the cabinet shut, and walked out.

Anja called after me, "I hope you puke on it, you self-righteous little *bastard*."

I gave most of the food to Jenny. The rest of it I divided up and shared out between the four of us. Russell was asleep, so I left his share on the bedside cabinet. Bird didn't want his, but I left it for him anyway. Fred just looked at the handful of manky old food and asked me where I'd got it from. I told him I'd found it down the back of the cooker. He didn't believe me, but he was too hungry to bother with the truth. He took the food and wolfed it all down in one go.

Friday, 9 March

First the good news.

There was a massive chunk of cooked meat in the lift this morning. A joint of roast beef on a silver platter. It looked beautiful. Thick, solid, juicy, succulent...

The smell of it was intoxicating.

And the bad news?

There were two sheets of paper pinned to the meat with skewers.

One of them was a grubby little note that we wrote about a month ago. Do you remember that secret meeting I told you about? The one with Russell and Fred? The one I wouldn't tell you about? Well, the reason I didn't want to tell you about it then was that I was worried The Man Upstairs might find out about it. But it doesn't matter now. Because He did find about it.

We wrote the note after Russell had told us everything he knew about the bunker. When Fred had first suggested his message-down-the-toilet idea, Jenny had been right to say that it was pointless sending a message if we didn't know where we were. But a bit later on, when I mentioned the idea to Russell, he pointed out that although we didn't know exactly where we were, we did have *some* information that was worth passing on.

We knew that we were probably somewhere in Essex.

We knew that we were still alive, and that as long as the police knew we were alive, they'd probably carry on looking for us.

And we knew that we were in an old nuclear bunker.

"There aren't that many of them around," Russell said. "And I know someone at Cambridge, a physicist called Dr. Lausche, who did some research on post-war nuclear facilities a few years ago. If I write out everything I know about this place, and we include an instruction with our note to pass these details on to Dr. Lausche, it's possible that he might be able to work out where we are."

So we'd written a note. Names, descriptions, best guesses . . . as much information as we could think of. And we'd carefully wrapped the note in several layers of black polythene torn from a bin liner, and we'd tied the bundle with brightly coloured plastic strips ripped from food packaging. And then we'd flushed the package down the toilet.

That was almost four weeks ago.

And now here it was. Returned to sender. Skewered to a piece of meat.

I think we all knew from the beginning that the chances of the note actually reaching anyone were virtually non-existent, and ever since we flushed it away I've been doing my best not to think about it, but I suppose in the back of my mind I've been clinging to the hope that someone would find it. So when I saw the note this morning, and when I realized what it meant, it hit me like a cold hard slap in the face.

If anything though, the other sheet of paper pinned to the meat was even worse. A printed note, it simply said:

lISTEN—mY WORD:
hE WHO KILLS aNOTHER SHALL BE fREe

We all looked at it for a long time. Ten words. Nine puzzled eyes. (Bird was still in his room.)

"Well?" I said eventually.

"Well what?" Fred answered.

"What does it mean?"

"Who cares?" He pulled out one of the skewers, speared it into the joint of beef, and dug out a big chunk of meat.

"Hold on," I said. "It might be drugged—"

"I don't care." He stuffed the meat in his mouth and started chewing. "I rahvver vee foison v'n 'ungry."

"What?"

"He said he'd rather be poisoned than hungry," Jenny said.

We watched him eat. Chomping, chewing, swallowing . . .

We looked at the meat. Mouth-watering, thick and juicy . . .

We looked at the note.

lISTEN—mY WORD:
hE WHO KILLS aNOTHER SHALL BE fREe

The meat won.

We went at it like hyenas, ripping out dirty great pieces with our bare hands and stuffing ourselves stupid.

Afterwards, when our bellies were full (and Russell and Jenny had been sick), we considered the note again.

lISTEN—mY WORD:
hE WHO KILLS aNOTHER SHALL BE fREe

"I think it's meant to be some kind of covenant," Russell said.

"What government?" said Fred, picking meat from his teeth.

"No," Russell said. "Not government. *Covenant*. It's a kind of contract. An agreement." He coughed weakly. "He's saying that if one of us kills one of the others, He'll free the killer. He'll let them go. A life for a life. That's His word."

No one said anything for a while. It was hard to know what to say. What with the other note, the food, and the strangeness of the message, we were all pretty mixed up. I looked at Russell. He had the note in his hand and was reading it very carefully. The paper was trembling in his hand. His face was puffy and pale. He put his hand to his mouth and coughed again.

"Yes," he said. "A covenant. I think that's it."

"I don't get it," I told him.

"It's simple," Russell explained. "If you kill one of us—me, for example—He'll let you go."

"Yeah, I understand that. I just don't understand why."

"Why what?"

"Why bother?"

"With what?"

"Why bother saying it?"

"Why not?"

"Because it's pointless. It's just stupid. He's not stupid. He might be stark raving mad, but He's not stupid."

"Stark staring," said Russell.

"What?"

His eye quivered. "It's stark *staring* mad. Not stark *raving*."

"Whatever. He's not stupid, is He?"

"No."

"He can't seriously believe we're going to start killing each other."

"No?"

"No."

Russell crossed his arms and shrugged. "Well, I don't think . . . I don't . . . " His voice trailed off and he started blinking. "I don't think . . . " His face stilled and he sat there staring into space. After a while his head began to sag and his eyes closed.

"Russell?" I said. "Russell . . . ? "

I leaned across the table and shook his arm. His head slumped forward and his breath rasped. He was miles away. Dead to the world.

"What's the matter with him?" Fred asked.

"Nothing," I said. "He's just tired. He'll be all right."

Fred shrugged. The message didn't seem to bother him at all. Neither did Russell's odd behaviour. Those kinds of things never bother Fred. It's like if he doesn't understand something, or if it doesn't have any direct relevance to him, he just ignores it.

It's not a bad way of going about things, I think. I wish I could do it.

Fred reached out, picked up the note and scanned the words. As he read, he carried on picking bits of meat from his teeth.

"It's crap," he said, tossing the note to the table. "He's just pissing around."

"Of course it's crap," I agreed.

"So why are we talking about it?"

"It says *he*," Jenny said suddenly.

I looked at her.

"The note," she said, pointing. "Look. It says *he* who kills another."

"It doesn't mean anything, Jen. Don't worry about it. It's just another of His stupid games."

"She's right," said Anja.

"What?"

"*He* who kills another. Not *the person* who kills another, or *she* who kills another."

"So *what*?" I snapped.

"That's what it says."

"So?"

She glared at me. "You're the one who said He's not stupid. If He's not stupid . . . " She began twisting a lock of hair round her finger. "If He's not stupid, why would He *say* that? Why would He?"

"Because He's mad. That's why."

She pouted at me.

I closed my eyes.

This is what He wants, I thought. *This* is what He wants. Madness, disruption, descent into chaos. This is what it's all about. He's like a little kid poking a stick into a nest of ants. He enjoys seeing the chaos.

That's it, isn't it?

That's what You want.

You just want to see what happens.

All right, I'll show You what happens. I'll write it down for You, OK? How about that?

What happens is this.

Bird comes out of his room and shuffles over to the table,

holding his head to one side and squinting at the light. His skin is a mess of blotches and streaks. He sits down.

"Hey," says Fred.

Bird grunts.

Despite the cold, he's sweating.

He looks at the meat.

"What's that?"

"What's it look like?" says Fred.

Bird glances at him. "What?"

Fred grins and shakes his head.

"Is he poorly?" whispers Jenny.

I nod.

Jenny looks at Bird with the true concern of a child. She shouldn't, but she does. With delicate fingers, she picks a shred of meat from the joint and offers it to Bird. He looks at her, sniffs, then plucks the morsel from her fingers and puts it in his mouth. Chews wearily. Swallows. Winces.

"There's a note," Anja tells him.

"Uh?"

She picks up The Man's note and passes it to Bird. He stares at her. Unsettled, she lowers her eyes. He reads the note. Blinks. Reads it again. Looks up. Blinks again. Then he carefully folds the note and puts it in his shirt pocket.

"I'm tired," he says. He stands up and groans. "My throat hurts."

Across the table Russell has opened his eyes and is staring intently at him. Bird looks back at Russell, says, "What?" then turns away and walks unsteadily back to his room.

All these things—the meat, the message, the £10 note folded into a butterfly—I've thought about them. I've thought long and hard. Are they supposed to mean something? Are they clues, symbols, signs, hints?

I don't think so.

They're just toys. Games. He's just messing about. That's all. He's just enjoying Himself.

I've thought about that too.

But I'm not going to tell you what I think just yet. Because 1) I'm not sure it makes any sense. And 2) If it does make sense, I'm not sure I want to talk about it.

Later on I made some tea and took it into Russell's room. It didn't smell too good in there. Kind of sicky and stale and a bit shitty, like a mad old person's room. Everything seemed dirty and brown, even the air.

Russell propped himself up on the bed and sipped his tea. Some of it dribbled down his shirt. He didn't seem to notice. I sat down and looked at him. He looks very old now. Ancient. Grizzly and weak. His black skin is tinged with yellowy-grey.

"Have you got it?" he said.

"Got what?"

"Have you worked it out yet?"

"I don't know what you mean."

"Come on, Linus," he sighed. "It's obvious. You've got a choice. One or the other. It's not going to be easy, of course, but it's all you've got. Believe me." His voice was short and breathy. He put down his tea and looked at me. "Are you up to it?"

I shook my head. "I'm sorry, but I really don't know what you're talking about."

"The note," he said. "The covenant. It gives you a choice. You have to..." His voice broke into a wet cough—*eck eck eck*—and flecks of spit splattered his lips. He wiped his mouth and went on. "You have to use what you've got, Linus. You turn the bad to good. Understand? Use what you've got..."

"What have I got?"

"Ah..." He raised a knobbly finger and waggled it absently in the air. His mouth was smiling loosely and his good eye was unfocused. It was too much to bear. I looked away, embarrassed. I didn't know what to say or where to look or how to feel. The room was silent and white. I stared at the floor, looking for something to look at, looking for patterns in the concrete, anything.

"Listen," Russell said suddenly. "You've got me or Bird. Two of us. We're both dying anyway. Take your pick."

"I don't—"

He waved me quiet. "I've had it, Linus. I've had enough. This thing..." He touched his head. "This thing is eating me. I can see it growing inside my head. I can *see* it. It changes shape. Like a coal-black finger, thin and crooked. Like a burnt stick of coral. Like a witch-bone. Like a blackened worm dried in the sun. Sometimes it's white, the white of fish-gristle. Or pink, like wet strings of chicken meat. I can see it. It's nothing. Rogue cells, that's all it is. Living bits gone wrong. Deformed misfits. Microscopic barbarians. Juvenile delinquents screwing themselves into oblivion." He laughed. "They're devoted to death, the little devils. They'll kill me and die doing it." He looked up. "You can't help but admire that, can you?"

"You're not making sense."

"Precisely," he said. "That's why..."

"Why what?"

"Never mind." He blinked hard. "Mr. Bird is infected. I don't know what it is. Dog germs ... probably septicaemia or meningitis or something. I don't know. I'm not a doctor. It doesn't matter. He's dying. Probably got a few days at most. So there you are. Two of us, dead already. You only need the one."

It began to dawn on me what he was saying. "You mean ... ?"

"Yes, *yes*," he grinned. "You cheat Him at His own game. Kill me or Bird, or both of us if you want, and He'll let you go. You can go home, go back to your father, then get the others out, Jenny, Fred ... " He glanced slyly at the camera on the ceiling and lowered his voice. "He doesn't know that we're dying anyway ... He doesn't *know* ... "

I felt like crying.

Crying for Russell's mind.

For mine too.

I let him carry on for a while, babbling on about the philosophy of death, natural justice, time and physics, until at last his head started sagging again and his eyes began to close and the words dried up. A dribble of spit had collected in the corner of his mouth. I went over and wiped it away and covered him up with a blanket. Then I walked sadly back to my room.

And here I am.

Lost.

My balance has gone.

The stuff I was thinking about earlier, about Him Upstairs enjoying Himself ... it's true. That's what He's doing. He's just enjoying Himself. And the thing is, it doesn't matter what I think about it. It doesn't matter what anyone thinks about it. Comprehension, judgement, disapproval ... none of it matters.

All that matters to Him is His enjoyment. Because He's all there is. Nothing else comes into it. It's Him alone. What He wants, what He needs, what He does. It's all beyond question.

That's all there is to it.

See?

I told you it was a waste of time thinking about it.

We finished off the meat this morning. Stupid, really. We all know we're not getting any more. We all know we should have saved it, been sensible, used our brains. But our brains seem to have gone on strike. We're living like animals now. Living on needs. Eat, drink, breathe, get through the day.

Tomorrow? What's tomorrow?

Today's tomorrow.

Today the lift is empty.

Tomorrow, too.

Bird went crazy at Jenny this afternoon. She was in the kitchen, she told me, getting a drink of water. Bird came in, mumbling to himself and shielding his eyes from the light, and walked over to the far wall. He didn't seem to notice Jenny at first. He just stood there looking at the wall for a while, then jerked his head and started waddling around the kitchen swearing at things.

"Waddling?" I said.

"Like this . . ." Jenny showed me, walking around with her knees bent and her feet sticking out. "Like a duck."

"A duck?"

"Yeah. He was walking around like that and then he just stopped in the middle of the kitchen and looked at the floor. His eyes were all wide and starey. Then he started stamping his feet and going on about wasps, and then he stopped again and just stared."

"*Wasps?*"

"I think so. It was a bit hard to understand what he was saying. He was talking all funny, like he had a wet mouth. I *think* it was wasps."

"What did you do?"

"I went over and offered him a drink of water. He went *mad*, Linus. Knocked the cup out of my hand and yelled at me, then pushed me away."

"Did he hurt you?"

"No, he just pushed me. Then he waddled out."

She's staying with me tonight.

She told me a joke. This duck goes into the chemist's. It goes up to the make-up counter and says, "I'd like a tube of lipstick, please. And would you put it on my bill."

Duck = 29.

Wasp = 30.

The world keeps turning.

Monday, 12 March

It's been a long day. Full of cold and hunger. Everything is that much harder without food. Hunger is a slow and lowering thing. It creeps up on you. You lose strength, and you lose heart. And the cold saps your energy, saps your will to do anything. Not that I've got much will left anyway. Whatever *will* is. Hope, determination, optimism, grit . . .

Words.

The cold gets into your bones and drains the life from your blood. It *hurts*. I've been cold before. I know what it's like. I've been cold and hungry before. I know what *that's* like. But knowing what something's like doesn't make it any easier. You just know what it's like.

And besides, it's different down here. Down here, the cold is . . . I don't know. It's just different. Colder than cold. Underground cold. Everywhere. Unrelenting.

Jenny can't stand it. It makes her cry.

This morning we ripped up a bible and lit a fire on the floor. Just a small one. Nothing fancy. Just a ragged pile of crumpled pages arranged in a circle. I lit it with Fred's cigarette lighter.

Click, crackle.

The magic of fire.

The flames were just beginning to flicker when the grille in the ceiling started to hiss and a fine spray of water came raining down. Jenny shrieked and cowered against the wall and I just sat there, soaking wet and freezing cold, watching the flames splutter and die.

After a few minutes the water stopped.

The half-burned bible pages were slopped in a puddle on the floor.

I looked up at the grille. Water was dripping slowly from the mesh—plip plip . . . plip . . . plip—like tears from a metal eye.

Murder beat in my heart.

Later on the noise started. That infernal racket he tortured us with before, the drums, the screeching, the wailing—shaking the walls, shaking our bones, making us weep and hold our heads and curl up on our beds like babies.

It lasted a long time, but it's over now.

A woman once told me how to deal with scary things. She was a psychiatrist, or a psychotherapist or something. I don't know. Is there a difference? Doesn't matter. She was one of those whispery women, all calm and relaxing. Long skirt, pale face, pale lips. She wore a small polished stone on a piece of string around her neck. Black and shiny, egg-shaped. I asked her what it was for. She said it helped to dissipate negative energy. Yeah, right, I thought. Negative energy. A polished stone . . . *that's* going to work, isn't it? That's really going to help.

Anyway, what she told me was . . .

Let me think.

It was something to do with unresolved fears.

Yeah, I remember.

She said, "Imagine something that frightens you, Linus. Something that's going to happen, say. A situation. Something you're worried about. Can you do that for me?"

"Yes."

"Good. Are you doing it now?"

"Yes."

"OK, now imagine that you can fly."

"Fly?"

"Like a bird."

"Ri-ght . . ."

"You can fly into the future."

"The future?"

"You can do it, Linus. All you have to do is fly up into the air . . . fly into the future, and then look down and *see* yourself in the situation you're worried about. You're there, right now. You're *in* this situation. Do you understand? You're there. Are you there?"

"Yeah," I lied.

"Good. Now look down at yourself. You can see yourself . . . you're there. See? It's all right. You're coping. Do you see? It's not so bad, is it?"

I couldn't work out whether to nod or shake my head. So I did something in between, a kind of diagonal, side-to-side nod. It didn't make any difference, there was absolutely nothing in my mind anyway.

Whispery-woman carried on. "Now, fly on a bit more, a bit further into the future, and imagine yourself when it's all over. You've been through this worrying situation and now everything is all right. Look, you can *see* yourself. You're fine. You can feel yourself . . . feel yourself, Linus. It feels OK, doesn't it?"

"Mmm."

"Good. Now, soak up that feeling, soak it right up into your body and remember it. Remember how it feels. Now turn round and fly back to *now*, all the time keeping that good feeling inside you. OK?"

"OK."

She smiled. "That's it. That's all you have to do, Linus. Look forward, *see* yourself feeling good, soak it up and remember it. Remember the future. Remember how it feels, and it'll be all right."

"What if it's not?" I said.

"Pardon?"

"What if I look forward and it's *not* all right? What if I'm *right* to be worried?"

"Ah," she smiled reassuringly, "but it *will* be all right. You have to make it all right."

"But—"

"Look, let me go over it again . . . "

I gave up in the end. Stopped listening. Tuned out. Yeah, right, yeah, I see, OK, great . . .

And that was that.

I don't know what time it is now. Probably about 10 or 11 at night. To tell you the truth, I'm too scared to go outside and look at the clock. There's a lot of bad stuff going on. Jenny is with me, and we've got the chair jammed up against the door.

Bird's been at it all night—screaming, swearing, stomping about, jabbering away like a lunatic. I saw him earlier on, about an hour after he'd gone loopy with Jenny. I was heading down the corridor towards the bathroom and he was just standing in his doorway, watching my every step. His face was a horrible shade of red, almost purple, and his skin was stretched as tight as a drum.

"Lye-nus," he drawled, his voice all slurred. "Hey, Lye-nus. Wanna see this?" He grinned a horror-grin and tugged violently at the open wound on his neck. His fingers bloodied. He licked at them, jabbed a crooked finger at me, and started chanting: "Linus Linus Linus Linus..."

I walked away, my heart beating hard.

Fred came to see us later.

"Stay in here," he said. "Keep the chair against the door. Bird's having a whack attack."

"It's the dog bite," I said. "He's got blood poisoning or something."

"Yeah, I know. Just stay in here, OK? He's been reading that stupid note. You know, the killing note. He just keeps reading it, over and over again. I don't think he'll actually do anything, but you never know."

"What about you?"

"Me?" Fred grinned. "You don't have to worry about me. I'm invincible."

"Where's Russell?"

"Barricaded in his room."

"Anja?"

Fred shook his head. "She keeps trying to talk to Bird. She thinks she can reason with him. I told her it wasn't safe, but she wouldn't listen. You know what she's like."

An image of Anja suddenly flashed into my mind, the Anja of six weeks ago. A confident-looking woman dressed in a sheer white top, short black skirt, tights, and high heels. Late twenties, well-spoken, honey-blonde hair, fine nose, sculpted mouth, perfect teeth, silver necklace. It was a far cry from the Anja of today—skinny, wretched, shabby and dirty, holed up in a stinking white room . . .

The trouble with people like Anja is they have no sense of danger. They don't know what fear is. They spend all their lives cocooned in comfort, and the only fears they ever know are the small ones—worries, anxieties, trifles. Anja has probably never had to be afraid before, not *really* afraid. And if you don't know how to be afraid, you're in trouble.

Fear serves a purpose.

It's not just for watching spooky films or riding rollercoasters. It's there for a reason.

It keeps us alive.

It's getting on for midnight now. Fred's gone. Jenny's asleep. I'm sitting against the wall, listening to the expectant silence and wondering what's going to happen. I know something's going to happen. I can feel it in the air. It's just a matter of what and when.

It's quiet outside.

The silence hums.

It's going to be a long night.

Wednesday, 14 March

So much has changed since I last wrote.

So much.

I don't know where to start.

It's unbelievable.

Maybe when I write it all down it'll make some sense.

I'll start at the beginning.

Tuesday morning, just gone eight o'clock.

The coldest day yet.

I'm lying on the floor, too cold to sleep, but too cold to get up. My stomach hurts. I raise my head and look around. Jenny's bed is empty. I don't know where she is. I suppose she's in the bathroom, or maybe the kitchen. We still have a few tea bags left. She's probably making a nice hot drink. I rest my head on the pillow and imagine cupping the tea in my hands, breathing in the steam, sipping the liquid heat . . .

And then the door opens and Jenny comes in, tea-less and agitated.

"Get up, Linus!" she says. "Quick, get up."

"Uh? What—?"

"Come on, hurry!"

Her face is white and her eyes are shocked.

I sit up. "What's the matter, Jen? What is it?"

"Anja," she says, and her voice breaks into breathy sobs. "I don't know... Fred said... she was... she's..."

I get out of bed and put my arms round her. "Hey, come on. It's all right—"

"No it's *not*."

"What's the matter? Tell me, Jenny. What is it?"

She can't speak, she's too upset. She can't stop crying. I hold her for a while then gently sit her down.

"All right," I say. "You stay here, OK? I'll go and see what's happening. I won't be a minute."

I leave the room and shut the door. Down the corridor, outside Anja's room, Fred and Russell are talking quietly. As I approach them, they stop talking.

"What's going on?" I ask them.

They look at me with grim faces.

Fred says, "Where's Jenny?"

"In my room."

He nods, then elbows Anja's door open. "You'd better take a look."

I go inside.

Anja is lying face up on the bed. Naked. Her throat is ringed with heavy bruising and her face is discoloured and swollen.

She's dead. Strangled.

"Shit," I say.

Fred and Russell come in and stand beside me.

Fred says, "I found her like that about ten minutes ago."

I look around the room. It's a mess. Sheets and pillows on the floor, dirty clothes all over the place, the bedside cabinet knocked over.

I shake my head, too numbed to know how I feel.

Russell puts his hand on my shoulder. It feels as light as a feather.

"Where's Bird?" I say.

"Here."

I turn round. Bird is standing in the doorway. He's barefoot and dressed in his suit. Underneath the suit he has a sheet wrapped around his chest. His head is tilted stiffly to one side, almost resting on his shoulder. He's staring past me at Anja's body, his eyes full of nothing.

I look questioningly at Fred. "What happened?"

He scratches his head and sniffs. "I don't know. I was up until six this morning. Didn't see anything. Didn't hear anything."

"Then what? After six?"

"I don't know. I fell asleep."

I look at Bird. "Did you do this?"

He doesn't answer me.

"Hey, Bird."

He blinks and looks at me. "Hmm?"

"Did you kill her?"

"Did I what?"

"Did you kill Anja?"

"Me?"

"Yes, you."

He cricks his neck and twists his mouth into an unnatural smile. "Why would I kill her? She loved me." He grins, staring at me. "And besides, it's not *me* who's got a proh-per-pensity for vi-oh-lensss, is it? I mean, who's the street-fighting man round here, eh? Is it me?" He shakes his head. "I don't think so, do you? I don't think it's *me* that goes round—"

Fred steps forward and hits him hard in the belly. Bird groans and sinks to the floor.

Next thing, we tie his hands with a belt. Then me and Fred wrap Anja's body in a sheet and drag it out to the lift. It's about eight-thirty now. The lift isn't down yet, so we leave the body by the door.

Fred grabs hold of Bird and we go down the corridor and gather at the table. Bird has clammed up now. Hasn't said a word since Fred hit him. His mouth is clamped shut and his jaw clenched tight. His face is alive with twitches. His skin is trembling.

"You know," Russell says, "he probably didn't know what he was doing. In the state he's in, he's not really accountable for his actions."

"So what?" says Fred.

Russell shrugs. "I was merely saying—"

"Well don't."

Russell looks like a living dead man. Colourless, frail, spiritless. There's nothing left of him.

"What are we going to do?" I say.

No one answers.

I look at Bird, then at Russell. "How long has he got?"

"Who?"

"Bird. How long has he got?"

"I don't know," Russell says. "I'm not a doctor. I don't even know what's the matter with him."

"You said he was infected—"

"No. I said as long as he *doesn't* get infected he should be OK."

"But he's not OK, is he? He's sick and crazy."

"I wouldn't say that, exactly. He may be suffering from some kind of personality disorder . . . his symptoms may be exacerbated by the pain and infection of the wound—"

"I wish you'd shut up," says Fred.

We all lapse into silence.

At this point I'm still trying to get my head round what's going on. I don't understand it at all. The cold shock of death, this strange aftermath, full of confusion . . .

And as I'm thinking about that, something really strange starts happening to me. I suddenly find myself—or some weird part of myself—floating up out of my body . . . up, up, up . . . and when I get to the ceiling I kind of twist around, and then I'm looking down at the scene below. I'm looking down at four tattered figures slumped round a table. Four barely-human beings, all dirty and tired, with sunken eyes and sick-looking skin. I see a big man with thick brown hair and a raggedy beard. I see a skeletal old black man, his skin hanging loosely off his frame. I see a bloated man with his hands tied together, dressed in a lunatic suit, all crazy and twisted. And I see a boy, a pathetic-looking thing with ropy hair and junkie skin and the baggiest clothes in the world.

And I think to myself—what are these people *doing*?

Well, says a voice in my head, *three of them are discussing the presumed act of the fourth. Three of them—a villainous drug addict, a dying man, and a vagrant kid—are discussing what to do about a purple-skinned fat man who they assume has murdered a rather distasteful woman.*

And with that thought I float back down into my body just in time to realize that we're all just sitting there, so wrapped up in our own futility, that we haven't noticed Jenny coming out of my room and crossing over to the lift. We haven't done anything to prevent her from seeing the sheet-wrapped corpse on the floor. And I hate myself for that.

I don't hate myself for much, but I hate myself for that.

We're all just sitting there, lost in our own sick heads, and poor Jenny's standing alone with a dead body under a sheet.

And then the lift comes down.

G-dung, g-dunk, whirr, clunk, click, nnnnnnnnn ... nnnnnnnnnnnnnnn ... g-dunk—mmm-kshhh-tkk.

I get up and go out into the corridor and my heart stops at the sight of Jenny stepping into the lift. She stoops down, picks something up, and steps out again holding a piece of paper. She reads it. Looks up, looks over at me, smiles awkwardly, then glances at the shape under the sheet, comes over to me, and hands me the sheet of paper. I see printed words.

I look at Jenny. "Are you all right?"

She nods.

"You sure?"

She nods again.

I smile at her, then read the note.

It says:

LiES—mY TRUTH:
LiNUS sLAYEd thE lADy

I read it again. And again, and again. And all I can think is— *what? WHAT?* And then my brain kicks in and I think—shit, what am I going to do with this? Tear it up? Screw it into a ball and eat it? Or do I put my trust in the others? Russell,

Fred, Jenny...do I have enough faith in them to trust me? Do they have faith in me? Do they *trust* me?

Of course they do.

Jenny follows me back to the table. We sit down and I pass the note to Russell. He reads it, looks at me, then passes the note to Fred. Fred reads it, looks at me, throws the note on the table.

"Well?" I say to no one in particular.

"Well what?" says Fred.

"What do you think?"

"About what?"

"The note, for Christ's sake. What do you think?"

"What do you *think* I think?"

I shake my head.

He says, "It's bollocks. Bullshit. You should be ashamed of yourself for even asking."

A tingle rises in my throat.

But then Russell says, "Now, hold on a minute..."

And that's when he starts jabbering on about stuff—justice, guilt, truth, innocence...the need for objectivity. At first I just assume there's nothing to it, he's just rambling. He's confused, sick, he doesn't know what he's talking about.

"We mustn't jump to conclusions," he says. "We have to listen to all sides of the argument. We have to lay aside our emotions and limit ourselves to the facts. And we *have* to consider the words of a witness, even if we mistrust his intentions. We have a duty to consider his testimony—"

"What *witness*?" Fred says. "What are you talking about?"

Russell says nothing, just looks up slowly and points at the ceiling.

Fred frowns, not getting it.

I still don't get it either, but then a worrying thought suddenly creeps into my head.

I look down at the note on the table.

LiES—mY TRUTH:
LiNUS sLAYEd thE lADy

"Is this what you're talking about?" I ask Russell, picking up the note. "Is this what you mean by 'the words of a witness'?"

Russell just looks at me, and it's clear from his silence that I'm right.

"Oh, for God's *sake*," Fred snorts, suddenly getting it. He glares at Russell. "You *are* joking, aren't you?"

"I've never been more serious in my life," Russell says.

Fred snorts again, shaking his head in disbelief.

Russell goes on. "Look, I'm not saying we have to *believe* His testimony—"

Fred laughs dismissively.

Russell remains calm. "Who else apart from the killer saw what happened?"

Fred shakes his head again. "This is ridiculous. Linus didn't kill Anja, for Christ's sake."

"I'm not saying he did. All I'm saying is . . ."

As Russell and Fred carry on arguing (and Jenny slopes off quietly to my room), I just sit there in silence, too miserable and bewildered to do anything. I know that Russell's lost his mind, and I know he doesn't know what he's doing, but that doesn't make it any easier to accept. He's doubting me. Sick or not, he's doubting me. And that hurts. So I just sit there, not really listening to him any more, just trying to empty myself of all the bad stuff I'm feeling . . .

And then another thought creeps into my head, a questioning voice that says:

Maybe he does know what he's doing?

Or at least, he thinks he does.

Maybe he thinks he's trying to help you?

And then I start thinking about the other note, the killing note—

lISTEN—mY WORD:
hE WHO KILLS aNOTHER SHALL BE fREe

—and I remember when Russell tried to persuade me to go along with it. All you have to do, he'd told me, is "Kill me or Bird, or both of us if you want, and He'll let you go." And now I'm thinking that maybe the reason Russell is trying to convince Fred and The Man Upstairs that I killed Anja is because he thinks it'll get me out of here.

In his twisted state of mind, he actually *believes* that Anja's killer will be freed, and he thinks (in his madness) that if he can persuade both Fred and The Man Upstairs that I'm the murderer The Man Upstairs will let me go.

But, of course, The Man Upstairs *knows* it wasn't me. He sees everything, he knows everything. He *is* the only witness. And He's not going to let anyone go anyway.

But Russell can't see that. His brain is all messed up, his reasoning has gone. He's lost it.

But I don't want to say that.

I don't want to say to Fred, "Hey, don't listen to this crazy old man. He's sick in the head. His brain is mangled."

No, I don't want to say that. It wouldn't be right.

So I just sit there, not hurting quite so much any more, and wait for Russell to talk himself out.

After a long twenty minutes or so, he begins to lose track of what he's saying. His twisted logic becomes even more twisted, he starts getting really confused—mumbling, muttering, rambling incoherently—and eventually he ends up just sitting there, staring at the table, his mouth hanging open and his poor face lost in bewilderment.

"I'll take him back to his room," I tell Fred.

Fred nods.

I take Russell back to his room, get him into bed, then go back to the table.

"What's the matter with him?" Fred asks me.

I tell him about Russell's brain tumour.

"He knows I didn't kill Anja," I explain. "He's just got this mixed-up idea that if The Man Upstairs believes I killed her, He'll let me go."

Fred nods. "I kind of guessed that."

I sigh.

Bird makes a horrible rasping sound then, hawking up something from the back of his throat. Me and Fred both look at him. He stares straight ahead, his left eye twitching.

"What the hell are we going to do with him?" I ask Fred.

Fred says nothing, just shakes his head.

We couldn't decide what to do with Bird. We secured him in his room, tying him to the bed, and then we just sat down and talked things over for hours and hours, trying to work out what to do. We didn't know why Bird had killed Anja, or whether he'd known what he was doing or not, and—as Fred pointed out—we didn't even know for sure that he *had* killed her.

"We're only guessing it was him," he said.

"Who else could have done it?"

"Russell."

I stared at Fred.

He shrugged. "It's possible, isn't it? He's not himself any more, he's half-crazy . . . he could have done it."

"No," I said, shaking my head. "No way."

Fred shrugged again. "You don't *know* that."

"Yeah, I do."

Fred was right, of course. I didn't *know* that Russell hadn't killed Anja. I was 99 percent sure that he hadn't, and I think Fred felt the same, but we couldn't discount the possibility. So then we had to try to work out what to do about that as well.

We didn't get very far.

How could we prove anything? How could we prove that Bird had done it, or that Russell had done it? And even if we could prove anything, what did we do then? Put the killer on trial? Punish him? Lock him up?

He was already locked up. We all were.

In the end, we got to the stage where we just couldn't think about it any more. We were too tired, too confused to carry on. It was early evening by then, and we'd been talking all day. We decided to leave it for now, get some rest. Start again tomorrow.

It happened in the early hours of the morning.

I was asleep in my room with Jenny, Fred was outside in the corridor. Bird and Russell were both in their rooms. Bird was still tied up—his belt-bound hands secured to the bed by another belt—but we hadn't done anything to restrain Russell. He was so weak now he could barely walk. I'd had to help him to the bathroom earlier on. He had no idea where he was or what he was doing. And besides, Fred was going to spend the night sitting in a chair at the kitchen-end of the corridor, so even if Russell did leave his room for any reason, Fred would see him. At least until the lights went out. And then he'd hear him.

"And I've still got this," Fred said, grinning and clicking one of the cigarette lighters The Man had sent down to us a million years ago. "Don't worry, Linus," he said, patting my shoulder. "Nothing's going to happen. You and Jenny get some sleep and we'll talk again in the morning."

I was confused when the sound of the lift woke me up. *G-dung, g-dunk.* It was dark, and it felt early. And that wasn't right. The lift comes down at nine o'clock. The lights are always on at nine o'clock. The lift doesn't come down when it's dark.

I sat up, rubbed my eyes, and listened.

Whirr, clunk, click, nnnnnnnnn . . .

It was definitely the lift.

I wasn't dreaming.

Jenny was still asleep. I could hear her sleepy breathing. I got up quietly, tiptoed across the pitch-black room, and opened the door.

"Fred?" I whispered into the darkness.

A light came on over by the lift, the flickering flame of

Fred's cigarette lighter. He was standing in front of the lift door, his head angled to one side, as if he was listening to something.

The lift came to a halt—*g-dung, g-dunk*.

The door didn't open.

"What's going on?" I asked Fred, crossing over to him.

"Listen," he said.

I listened. Silence.

"It's stopped now," Fred said.

"What's stopped?"

"It sounded like a phone ringing."

"Where? In the lift?"

He nodded. "I could have sworn—"

A phone started ringing.

"There it is!" Fred said. "I knew I'd heard it."

It was an old-fashioned telephone ring—*brrr, brrr . . . brrr, brrr*. I stepped closer to the lift door and listened hard. There was no doubt it was coming from inside the lift.

"What's He doing?" I said.

Fred shook his head. "God knows."

The ringing stopped.

Nothing happened for a moment.

And then suddenly—*mmm-kshhh-tkk*—the door opened and the phone started ringing again. We could see it now. It was on the floor at the back of the lift. A cheap-looking mobile with a grubby white casing. The screen was flashing on and off with the ringtone.

Brrr, brrr . . . brrr, brrr.

Brrr, brrr . . . brrr, brrr.

"What do we do?" I said to Fred.

"Nothing," he said. "Just leave it."

"But it might be—"

"It won't be anything, Linus. He's playing games with us again. It's just another—"

All the lights came on then, a sudden flash of blinding white, and a second later we heard the scream. It came from behind us, from my room . . . from Jenny. I turned and ran.

"*JENNY!*" I yelled. "*JENNY!*"

My door was half open. I barged through it and saw Bird bending over the bed, trying to get hold of Jenny. She was scrabbling away from him, swatting away his hands, her face shocked white and her eyes wide with fear. I threw myself at Bird, got hold of him round the neck and started pulling him away. He twisted round and clawed at me like a lunatic—hissing and growling, spitting, snarling—and then suddenly Fred was there, grabbing hold of Bird's shoulders, swinging him round and hammering his massive head into his face. Once, *crack*. And again, *crack*.

Bird went down without a sound.

We still haven't worked out exactly how it happened. We know that Bird gnawed his way through the belts at some point because we found the chewed remains of them in his room, but the rest of it we can only guess at. We think The Man Upstairs must have been watching Bird (infrared cameras?). He must have seen him chewing through the belts, waited until he was almost free, then distracted us with the phone in the lift so we didn't see Bird sneaking out of his room. Of course, He couldn't have known what Bird was going to do, but it was

211

pretty obvious he was going to do something, and I guess that's all that matters to Him. As long as He's got something to watch He's happy.

God knows what Bird was actually doing.

Was he after me?

Did he know that Jenny was in my room?

I don't even want to think about it.

Jenny's just about OK now. She was badly shaken up for a while, but after I'd sat with her for an hour or so—telling her over and over again that there was nothing to worry about any more, that Bird was gone and she'd never see him again—she slowly began to come out of it.

"Is he really gone?" she asked quietly.

I nodded.

"Is he dead?"

I nodded again.

"Did Fred kill him?"

"I didn't mean to kill him, Linus."

"I know."

"I thought I'd just knocked him out. It wasn't till I'd dragged him out that I realized he was dead."

"You did what you had to do, Fred. He was probably just about dead anyway. Not that it matters. As long as Jenny's all right, that's all that counts."

I'm getting it all mixed up now. I can't remember if I talked to Fred first and then talked to Jenny, or if it was the other way round. All I know for sure is that at some point I was sitting at the table with Fred, and Jenny was in my room, and I suddenly realized that while all this craziness had been going on we hadn't seen or heard anything from Russell.

"We'd better go and check on him," I said to Fred.

I looked in on Jenny first. She was asleep—all curled up, nice and snug, sucking quietly on a finger. I closed the door and left her to it.

Fred followed me down the corridor to Russell's room.

I knocked on the door.

No answer.

I knocked again.

Still no answer.

I looked at Fred.

He shrugged.

I opened the door, just an inch.

"Russell?"

Nothing.

"Russell?"

The silence was ominous.

With a heavy heart, I pushed open the door and went inside. For a fraction of a second everything seemed normal—the walls, the floor, the ceiling, the bed—and then I saw him. He was lying on the bed wrapped in a reddened sheet.

The sheet was wet.

The red was blood.

My legs were shaking as I went over for a closer look. I sank down on to the bed, numbed to the bone. A hollow sickness ached in my belly.

You know what I thought then? I thought, *This is it. This is what happens and what will happen. This is where you're going,*

Linus. This—this silence, this stillness, this lack of feeling—this is where you're going.

When I looked into Russell's lifeless face, a flood of wretchedness filled my heart. I've never had a feeling like it before. Words can't describe it. Through cold tears I looked down at the empty socket where his glass eye should have been. Lying on the sheet beside his head was a splinter of coloured glass.

It took me a moment to get it.

Russell Lansing had popped out his glass eye, smashed it on the floor, and opened his wrists with a blue-and-white shard.

It's getting late now.

I've talked with Jenny, told her about Russell. I didn't tell her everything, but I didn't lie. I told her that Russell had cancer.

"A girl at school got cancer," she told me. "Carly Green. She died too. She got leukaemula from the power station."

"The *nucular* power station?"

Jenny smiled.

She's not stupid.

She asked me what's going to happen to us.

"I don't know," I admitted.

"Are we going to die too?"

"Nah," I said. "Not us."

"Why not?"

"Lots of reasons."

"Like what?"

"Weedy Power, for one."

"What else?"

"Well, for a start, Fred's invincible. Second, you're too smart. And third, I'm too pretty."

She laughed. "You're not *pretty*. *Girls* are pretty."

"Yeah? What am I then?"

"Pretty ugly," she giggled.

"Thanks."

"Pretty whiffy too," she added.

"And you're not, I suppose?"

Her face suddenly dropped.

"Hey," I said, "I didn't mean—"

"Yeah, I know."

She sniffed and wiped her nose. I felt bad then. Bad for the little things. It's not the big stuff that really gets to you, it's the little things. Things like cold bathrooms, dirty sheets, and little girls who have to put up with smelling bad.

Jenny looked up at me. "What's going to happen, Linus?"

"Nothing," I lied. "We're going to be all right."

I've got the others' notebooks—Anja's, Bird's, Russell's. I've been looking around their rooms too. I waited until Jenny was asleep and then I went nosing around. It was a bit spooky, and it didn't make me feel too great, but then I didn't feel too great anyway.

Anja's notebook is blank. Not a word. Nothing at all. It looks like it's never been opened. I thought that was quite sad at first—having nothing to say, no one to talk to, no secrets, no desire to leave anything behind. But then it struck me that maybe it wasn't such a bad thing after all. I mean, what's so great about sharing your thoughts with someone who doesn't exist? What good does it do? Where does it get you? Nowhere, as far as I can see. Nowhere useful anyway.

Her room had a peculiar smell to it. It smelled exactly how you'd expect a dirty posh woman's room to smell, a curious mixture of waste and wealth. A bit sweet and a bit sour. Like a dead flower. Or like a £50 note that's been in a tramp's pocket for a week. Not very nice, but not *too* bad either.

I found some more food in there. There wasn't much—a couple of crackers under the pillow, four rashers of cooked bacon hidden in the bible, a small furry lump of chocolate under the bed—but it's enough to keep us going for a few more days. The thought of Anja hiding it away didn't make me feel angry any more. It didn't make me feel anything, to be honest.

Bird's room was neater than Anja's. Not clean, but neat. Neat in a scary kind of way, as if he didn't move around much when he was in there, just lay on his bed staring at the ceiling thinking scary thoughts. Although it was neater than Anja's room, it smelled a lot worse. It smelled like fifty years of sweat and putrefaction. There were also one or two signs that Bird had lost it near the end. Urine stains on the wall, dried turds under the bed...

I took his notebook and got out of there.

The writing in his notebook is really hard to read, all cramped and scrawly, like he was drunk all the time. Apart from the records he kept of our meetings, it's mostly filled with strange little undated notes, each one written on a separate page. I'm not sure what any of it means. For example:

10.59
a11.25
13.00B
a1306

movement/time/wasted

Philp Satar 99273

7 down
7 Marlett
3

firedefinelinesignwhine

usleless

law = devolution (weakness)
law weakness
weakness is gaurded by law

152
1142

start with 1 ≢ 61 67 8 47 end 34

PICTURES?

pci peice pice pice peice

I left Russell's room until last. I didn't really want to go in there at all. He was dead, but his memory was alive, and I wanted to leave it at that. But something made me go in there. I don't know what it was, some kind of ghoulish curiosity, I suppose. Something stronger than sentiment.

The air smelled thick and coppery, almost salty, and there was a silence to the room that reminded me of the silence of a church. You know, like you're not supposed to be there, like something's watching you. I stood there for a while, just looking around, trying to breathe calmly. It wasn't easy. There were tiny splinters of coloured glass scattered on the floor by the bed, shining dully in the light. They looked like blue-and-white needles. The bed was still bloody and there were ugly smears on the floor where we'd dragged the body out. There was other stuff in there, too . . . stuff I don't want to talk about. It was all too much. I got his notebook from the cabinet and took it back to my room.

I've just finished reading it. Page after page of words and pictures and diagrams . . . there's all kinds of stuff in there. Thoughts, letters, theories, equations, drawings, even poems. It's incredible. Beautiful, dark, harrowing, complex, and indescribably sad.

I'm not going to show you any of it.

The last entry is addressed to me.

Dear Linus, it begins.

The rest is illegible, just a dying scrawl.

I'm going to sleep.

Sunday, 18 March

It doesn't take long to sink back into a routine. Whatever it takes, I suppose. You just take it, live it, hour after hour after hour.

07.00: You wake up shivering. It's impossibly cold. You can't get up. There's a nasty taste in your mouth and your tongue feels furry. You've got a throbbing headache and a stuffy nose. You're tired. You're not hungry, but you can't stop thinking about food. Cheese, honey, hot meat, green vegetables swimming in gravy. You don't even *like* vegetables. And fresh air too. You can't stop thinking of fresh air. Wind, sky, open spaces. Gardens, fir trees, hedges . . .

What do you do?

I lie in bed thinking of other times.

When I was a little kid. When Dad was home, telling me rhymes. I remember the one about budgies and crabs and grizzly bears, and the one with the buffaloes, and last night I finally remembered another one, a longer one. It was about a tortoise. I started thinking about it about three days ago, and last night I finally got it:

> *A rich lady tortoise called Joyce*
> *was driving her shiny Rolls-Royce,*
> *when a boisterous young oyster*
> *made a noise like a rooster*

Joyce crashed her shiny Rolls-Royce.
A kind little turtle called Myrtle
ran up and said, "Oh! are you hurtle?"
The tortoise replied, "I'm fine, thank you, Clyde,"
and Myrtle said, "Oh, but I'm Myrtle."
You see, Joyce had a husband called Clyde
whose face was quite turtle-ified,
so when Joyce was quite shaken
by the knock she'd just taken
she mistakenly thought Myrtle was Clyde.

I'm not sure though . . .

It doesn't quite work, does it?

I've probably misremembered it.

Anyway, there was another one. A shorter one, about a zebra, which I just can't remember at all. I've been racking my brains for days, but I can't get it. And that's really bothering me.

08:00: The light comes on and my memories fade. I get out of bed, already dressed, and wrap myself in blankets. Everything's cold, but my feet are the coldest. They're cold all the time. Drinking gallons of icy water probably doesn't help. I go to the bathroom, wash, slip the sheet over my head and try to use the toilet. Not much there. I walk back down the corridor, nod a silent greeting to Fred as he passes the other way, and go into the kitchen. Sit down, wait for the lift to arrive.

08:45: Jenny comes in. We talk. She has sores on her mouth and her nose is runny. Her breath smells horrendous. Mine too, I expect.

08:55: Fred wanders in, shirtless, scratching his belly. He doesn't say much. He ruffles Jenny's hair. I tell him I want to see him later. He says OK, drinks from the tap, and wanders back to his room.

09:00: The lift comes down. Empty.

09:30: The day drags on. I talk to Fred. We discuss how long we can go without food. Neither of us knows for sure, but we both think it's probably quite a long time. Ten days, a couple of weeks, a month . . .

"As long as we've got water," Fred says. "Water's what counts."

"Yeah."

"You got any ideas?"

"About what?"

"Getting out of here."

I look at him. I start giggling.

"Shit," he says.

My laughter turns to tears.

Later on, back in my room, I lie down and think some more about the zebra. It's becoming an obsession. *There once was a zebra . . .*? No. *Zebras are . . .*? No. I try to imagine Dad's mouth speaking the words, hoping it'll nudge my memory. I see his teeth, his lips, his bristly moustache . . . but I can't hear the words. And now I can't even remember what he looks like.

I can't remember what Mum looked like either.

No, hold on . . . there she is. I can see her now. We're walking down the road together, a long time ago. It's dusty. There are builders across the road, building a new house or something. I can hear the dumper trucks. Drills. The whump of a jackhammer. Shouts for tea. The road is tracked with dried clay and the clay is zigzagged with the tyre marks of the dumper trucks. Dried clay is good for kicking. Cracks off nice and hard.

Mum tugs at my hand. "On the pavement, please."

I pull away from her and aim another kick, and a slab of dried clay skids across the street.

"Linus!"

At the bottom of the road we pass a workman coming up. One of the builders. Knapsack, hat, cigarette, boots, a T-shirt over sun-browned skin. He's got a bracelet on his wrist, a silver snake. He steps aside to let us pass. Dark eyes, a passive nod. Then he carries on up the street. I look back at him, wondering what he is. He looks like an outlaw Indian from one of Dad's picture books. Blue Duck the Cherokee, or the Apache Kid. Yeah, the Apache Kid, took to the hills as a renegade, swooped down to pillage and rob from time to time, eluding all pursuers.

"Don't stare," Mum says. "It's rude."

"*You* were."

"I was *not*."

"You were. I saw you."

"Don't be stupid. Come on."

We turn the corner and go down the hill.

"Is he a bad man?" I ask.

"Who?"

"That man, the hat man."

"He's just a builder. He builds houses."

"Where does he live?"

"*I* don't know. Give me your hand, we're crossing here."

"Can I wear a hat?"

"Give me your hand." We cross the road.

"What's it called, Mum. On his arm?"

"What's what? Mind the dog dirt."

"The—"

"*Mind!* Watch where you're going."

I'm skipping now, making circling gestures on my wrist. "Here, on his arm. That man had a snake."

"A tattoo?"

"*No.*"

"What then?"

"Like a ring. Like a . . . you know . . . on his wrist."

"A ring? Oh, a *bracelet.*"

We stop again, hand in hand, opposite the newsagent's. Traffic is light, but Mum does it right: look right, look left, look right again, then walk—don't run—across the road.

"Can *I* get a snake bracelet?"

"No."

Last night I thought I had the flu or something. I woke up early in the morning feeling really bad. Kind of sick and hollow. My head was splitting and everything was aching like hell. Legs, arms, chest, even my eyes were throbbing. My nose was all bunged up with snot and I could hardly breathe. Then within an hour or so, I started feeling all right again.

Very odd.

I suppose it's just a lack of energy. No fuel, no energy. No energy, no good. No good, bad.

I've been looking for insects. Cockroaches, flies, spiders . . . whatever. Yeah, I know spiders aren't insects. I ain't dumb. You know what I mean. Bugs, creepy-crawlies, invertebrates, small crunchy things on legs. I've looked everywhere. Down the back of the cooker, along the walls, nooks and crannies. I couldn't find anything. Nothing. Not even a dried-up fly.

Where's all the bugs when you need them?

Escape seems to have drifted away. I don't think about it any more. What's the point? I don't want to get gassed. I don't want to get wet. I don't want my head bombarded with noise. All I want, most of the time, is to sleep.

I wonder what He did with the bodies. Anja, Bird, Russell, the dog . . . what's He done with them all? Buried them? Burned them? Chopped them up? Put them in bin liners and chucked them in a river? Maybe He's eaten them. That'd be something, wouldn't it?

Another thing I wonder about is His appearance. What does He look like? I can't remember. My memory of Him is useless. All I can remember is a blind man in a raincoat, and I know He's not that. A while ago I flipped back through the pages of this notebook and found Russell's description of Him. *Middle-aged, dark hair, about five feet ten inches tall. Well built, but not overly muscular. Strong hands. Clean-shaven. Lightly tinted spectacles. Charcoal suit, white shirt, burgundy tie. Black slip-on shoes, burgundy socks.*

It's a pretty good description, but it doesn't mean anything to me. It's not how I see Him.

That bothered me for a while. I didn't understand why I should have a different picture in my mind. Why should I reject the probable truth? But then I thought, why not? I can do what I like.

So this is how I see Him.

He's quite short, kind of dumpy, about forty years old. He wears plastic-framed glasses with greasy fingermarks on the lenses. The glasses keep slipping down His nose, and when He pushes them back up He wrinkles His upper lip. His skin is pale, sallow. He has a childish mouth, an unremarkable nose, and small round ears. His hair is shit-brown. He combs it to one side and thinks it looks smart, but it doesn't. Clothes? He wears pale-coloured nylon shirts with the sleeves always buttoned. No tie, suit trousers, slip-on shoes, a zip-up leather jacket from somewhere cheap like Peacocks or Primark.

How's that, Monster Man?

Am I close?

No?

Well, I'll tell You what. That's *my* picture of You, and that's all that counts. It doesn't matter what You think about it. All that matters is me. Because I'm all there is. Nothing else comes into it. It's me and me alone. What I imagine, what I see, what I think . . . it's beyond question.

That's all there is to it.

OK?

What I see is what You are.

Wednesday, 21 March

The lights come on.
  The empty lift comes down.
  The day passes.
  The empty lift goes up.
  The lights go off.

All my life I've never really felt like I belonged anywhere. Home, school, the street . . . wherever I've been, it's never seemed right. The street was OK while it lasted, but it was never really for me. I don't really have what it takes for the street. I got away with it for a while, but I know it would have found me out in the end. Home was always mixed up. Even when I was little, before Mum died, I never really felt happy at home. And school was even worse, especially after Dad got rich. The ordinary kids didn't like me any more because they thought I was rich, the rich kids didn't like me because they thought I was ordinary. I never knew where I was. And now here I am, stuck in the depths of this cold white bunker . . .

And you know what? I finally know how it feels to belong somewhere.

The three of us stay together most of the time now. We've moved all the mattresses and blankets into my room, all the sheets, everything. I don't know if it helps, but at least it gives the impression of being warmer. We lie around all day, huddled up in this tiny room, not doing much. Saving energy. Saving heat. Surviving.

Our skin is getting wrinkled and yellow. Our muscles are thin and stringy. We're cold all the time. We should have taken the others' clothes. They wouldn't have minded. Dead people don't need clothes.

Sometimes, when we're not too cold, we talk. It passes the time.

FRED: We should have kept the dog.

ME: What?

FRED: The dead dog, the Dobermann. We should have kept it. Put it in the fridge. We could be stuffing ourselves with fried dog now if we'd kept it.

ME (giving him a look): Christ, Fred . . .

FRED: What? Are you telling me you wouldn't eat a chunk of fried dog right now?

ME: Well, no . . . but—

FRED: It's no different to eating anything else. Chicken, cow, pig . . . it's all just meat. Flesh. Food. Energy. It's all the same. (He grins) We should have kept Bird and the others too. Bird would have kept us going for months.

ME (smiling): You're an animal, Fred.

FRED: We're all animals.

JENNY: I'm not an animal.

FRED (gently): Yes, you are.

JENNY: I'm not.

FRED: You are.

JENNY: Not.

FRED: Are.

Jenny, smiling, punches Fred on the arm. Fred cries out and grabs his arm, pretending he's hurt. He topples over and rolls around on the floor, writhing in mock agony.

We watch him for a while.

Eventually he stops, grins, and just lies there on the floor. We're all silent for a while.

Then:

JENNY (quietly, to me): Are you scared?

ME: I don't know. I suppose so. Yeah.

JENNY (to Fred): Are you scared?

FRED: No.

JENNY: Why not?

ME: He's too stupid.

FRED (giving me the eye): You're lucky I can't be bothered to get up.

ME: Yeah?

FRED: You want to know why I'm not scared?

ME: Not really.

FRED: I'll tell you why. (He props himself up into a sitting position) I've been in worse places than this before. I got out then, and I'll get out now.

ME: Places like what?

FRED: You don't want to know.

JENNY (to Fred): What's the scaredest you've ever been?

FRED (grinning again): Well, there was this one time . . . I was staying with some friends out in the country somewhere, I can't remember where it was. It might have been somewhere in Wales, or maybe Cornwall. Somewhere like that. Anyway, we were in this old stone cottage right out in the middle of nowhere, and I was in bed one night, fast asleep, and all I can really remember is suddenly waking up and seeing a monkey sitting at the bottom of my bed.

JENNY: A monkey?

FRED: It was just sitting there. Staring at me.

ME: Which one was it?

FRED: What?

ME: Which one of the Monkees? Davy Jones? Or was it the one with the funny hat?

FRED (laughing): Now, that *would* be scary.

Of course, Jenny doesn't get it. She's never heard of the Monkees. So then I have to explain who they are (a 1960s pop group who had their own TV series), and I have to explain why I know anything about a 1960s pop group (my dad loves them, he's got all their records), and by the time I've done that, my monkey/Monkee joke isn't funny any more.

And then we start talking about something else . . .

And the time drifts by.

Saturday

It's too tiring to write. Too depressing. It's bad enough feeling like this without having to write about it. I'll tell you one thing though—I'm sick of being hungry. It doesn't actually hurt any more, it doesn't cause me any violent suffering. In fact, the physical pain is hardly worth mentioning. Hunger is a longing rather than a suffering. But it's there all the time, boring away deep inside me like a worm. I hate it.

It's a hard feeling to describe.

Think how it feels when you haven't eaten for a while. Think empty. The pit of your stomach. The back of your throat. Dry and empty. Think of yourself shrinking.

Think a hundred times worse.

I don't think we can last much longer.

I think of you.

You and You.

I think of you, comfortable in your nowhere. Doing nothing. Existing, reading this, killing me. I'm never getting out of here. Never going to burn you. I give you what you are.

I think of You.

Whatever it takes, whatever it takes . . .

Promises.

Body. Air. Food. Water. Blood.
Eternity.
You think about that.

Sunday

I ate some pages from the bible. Stupid thing to do. Ripped them out, tore them into strips, chewed and swallowed them. They tasted papery. A bit inky. Not the greatest taste in the world, but as soon as the pages hit my stomach, my hunger exploded like you wouldn't believe. I started wolfing down more, stuffing the pages into my mouth two, three, four at a time.

And then the cramps set in. Stomach cramps. God, it hurt so much. I thought I was dying.

Spent the rest of the day suffering.

Sick, diarrhea, sick . . .

Tip for the day: never eat a bible when you're starving to death.

Monday

08:00: the lights come on.

09:00: the lift comes down.

I've got so used to it, I don't have to look at the clock. The hour is ingrained in my body. The sudden sterility of the lights, the silent click, then 60 minutes later the metallic sound of the lift—*g-dung, g-dunk* . . .

As dependable as the rising sun.

So when the lift didn't come down this morning, it felt like the end of the world.

Imagine how you'd feel if the sun didn't rise. Imagine that.

The three of us gathered in the corridor.

"Maybe the clock's wrong," Fred suggested.

"The lift *is* the clock."

He knew what I meant.

We stared at the closed door. Solid metal, silvery dull.

"Maybe it's broken," Jenny said. "Lifts are always breaking. My dad got stuck in one once. They had to wait for the fire brigade."

"I don't think He'll be calling the fire brigade." I looked at Fred. "What do you think? Is it broken?"

"How the hell should I know?"

We stood there for a while, just staring at the closed door, making the occasional comment.

"Maybe it'll come down later."

"Yeah."

"Doesn't really matter anyway..."

"No."

Of course, it *does* matter. The lift might be broken. And that could mean something, although I don't know what. Then again, it could be that He's just playing His stupid games again. Giving us something to think about. Shaking us up.

Seems a bit pointless though.

I mean, compared to what He's already done, and what He could do, it's a pretty crappy kind of game. Hardly worth the bother, really.

On the other hand—and this is what really matters—it could mean that He's not up there any more. Maybe He's gone. Just got fed up and left. Or He could be ill. Or He could be just pretending.

Yeah, that's more like it. That's a good game. Playing possum. Playing dead. He makes us think that He's gone, and when we try something—*BOOM!*—ha ha, fooled you all!

Very funny.

I'll have to think about that.

Talk it over.

First, though, I have to sleep. All this activity has tired me out. Standing up, walking, talking, writing... I'm exhausted.

Slept for a few hours. I don't seem to dream any more. Not that I remember anyway. It's about ten o'clock at night now. The lift still hasn't come down. I'm so cold, I think my blood has frozen.

We've talked about the possibilities.

What does it mean to us if the lift is broken?

What does it mean if it's not?

What does it mean to us if He's gone?

What does it mean if He's only pretending?

There was a lot to talk about.

Options, risks, outcomes.

Hopes, fears, maybes.

Optimism, pessimism, don't-get-too-excitedism.

It was hard work.

1) because we're all half-dead and can't think clearly.

And 2) because we have to assume He's still up there, watching and listening.

We used pens and paper to start with, but it was so time-consuming, so incredibly frustrating and tiring, that in the end we gave up. Instead, we covered ourselves in a tent of sheets and whispered to each other. There was a chance He'd gas us, or turn on the water, or the noise, but it was a chance worth taking.

Nothing happened.

We talked things through. From optimism to pessimism and back again. Finally we settled on somewhere in the middle.

We're going to wait.

Fred was against it at first. He wants to know if He's still up there or not, one way or the other. Right now.

"If He's not there we can do something. Do it right now. We don't have time to wait."

"But what if He is still there?"

"What have we got to lose?"

Our lives, I thought.

"All right," I said. "Let's just give it another day."

"*Why?*"

"We have to play to our strengths," I said. "We're weak, drained, confused, starved, cold. The only thing we're fit for is waiting. We've spent the last two months doing nothing. We're good at it. He's not. Let's use what we've got."

"Then what?"

"Then we do something."

Fred looked at me, his eyes struggling to stay open.

"OK," he said eventually.

We both turned to check that it was OK with Jenny, but she was already asleep.

Now I'm alone, with you, listening to the hum of the walls, and I'm beginning to doubt myself. I want to tell you something, but it's best if I don't.

Let's just say I can see the end of something, the end of a trail of doubts.

And it doesn't look good.

I wish I had something to read apart from the bible. I can't possibly read that. Anything else would do, anything to take my mind off thinking. A dictionary would be good. Yeah, a dictionary. If I had the choice between a chocolate cake and a dictionary...well, obviously I'd take the cake. But I'd have to think about it.

No I wouldn't.

I'd swap a thousand dictionaries for a piece of stale cake.

I would like a dictionary though. A dictionary contains all

the books ever written, and all the books that will ever be written. That's something, isn't it? The words aren't in the right order, of course, but it's still something.

You know what else I'd like?

A map of the world.

I'd pin it on the wall. Then I'd know where everywhere was. It'd be right there, on the wall.

I'm off to think about zebras now.

The lights are out. I don't know what time it is. The clock's stopped. It's 11:35 for ever. I'm writing this in the light of a fire.

Now we're starting down the trail of doubts.

I was in the kitchen when it happened. Jenny was asleep. Fred was in the bathroom. I'd just washed my face and I was peering at my reflection in the steel surface of the sink, trying to convince myself that I didn't actually look like that, that it was the paucity—I remember the word popping into my head—that it was the *paucity* of the sink as a mirror that was the problem, not me . . . or some such drivel.

Some such?

Paucity?

What's the matter with me? Why am I suddenly talking like a Charles Dickens character? Maybe I'm turning into Oliver Twist. Desperate with hunger and reckless with misery . . . please, sir, I want some more . . .

Anyway, I was stooped over the sink. Everything was as dull and deadly quiet as it always is. Boring, airless, flat, white. Suddenly I sensed something. I didn't know what it was. A vibration, perhaps. A shift in tone or pressure. A faint change in the unheard rhythm of the bunker . . . I don't know. Whatever it was, it didn't last long. A second, two at the most, and then the silence fell. Absolute silence. It sounded very loud for a moment, then incredibly quiet. I swear I could hear my blood running cold.

The humming had stopped.

That's what it was.

The humming in the walls. Stopped. Gone.

No power, I thought. *Shit, if there's no power . . .*

And that's when the lights went out.

The kitchen was blacker than black. Lightless. Sightless. As I stood there staring into the dark, a vision came to me of the very first morning I woke up down here. I saw myself getting out of bed and groping my way to the door and out into the corridor. Scared to death. Touching the walls. Scared of the dark. Tapping my foot on the floor. Scared of what I couldn't see. No clock, no hands, no sky, no sounds, just solid darkness and a low humming sound deep within the walls.

And now even the humming was gone.

I was nothing, existing in nothing.

"We shouldn't have waited," I said out loud.

My voice was a foghorn.

"Shit."

The next thing I did was possibly the stupidest thing I've ever done.

After I'd stood there for a while, listening to Fred's distant shouts from the bathroom—"Hey! What's going on? Where's the light? Hey! Linus? *Linus!*"—I suddenly realized that I was incredibly thirsty. I don't why. Maybe it was the adrenaline or something, sucking out my precious fuel reserves . . . I really don't know.

All I knew was that I had to have a drink, right now.

Without thinking, I turned on the tap, let it run, and started feeling around in the dark for a cup. But I couldn't find one. I felt along the draining board, along the counter, then reached up into the cupboards. I was panicking. You know how the dark can make you panic over stupid little things? Well, that's my excuse. I was panicking. I wasn't thinking. My hands were clattering through the cupboards, finding plates and bowls, but still no cups, and all the time the water was streaming from the tap, splashing into the sink, draining away, down the plughole . . .

And then three things happened simultaneously.

1) my hand closed on a cup

2) a thought flashed into my head—*save the water!*

and 3) the tap started coughing, spitting out the last few drops.

No power, no plumbing, no water.

Shit! No water!

I dropped the cup, crashed around in the sink looking for the plug, stuck my hand over the plughole, found the plug, dropped it, found it again, and stuck it in the plughole. But by then the water from the tap had dried up. The tap was silent. No hissing, no gurgling, no nothing. I groaned. I dried my hand on my shirt, groaned again, and put my hand in the sink. Hoping hoping hoping for a touch of water . . .

Please . . .

There was just enough to dampen my palm.

I need to rest now.

More later.

Later.

So there I am, in the kitchen, feeling dead and stupid and disbelieving. From the other end of the bunker I can hear Fred trying to flush the toilet. It brings a momentary smile to my face. He's always doing that. Pumping away on the handle, flush, flush, flush . . . only this time it sounds different. It sounds dry and empty . . . waterless.

Oh no.

"*Fred!*" I call out. "*Don't flush it! FRED!*"

But he's too busy trying to flush. He can't hear me.

I start running out of the kitchen, racing through the darkness . . . and run straight into the open door. *Whack!* I'm vaguely aware of the initial shock, a cracking sound, a dull thud, and for the tiniest fraction of a second I think—*it's OK, I'm all right, I just ran into the door, that's all, it's not so bad*—and then the truth kicks in with a blinding roar that sears through my head and I stagger drunkenly to one side and fall to the floor clutching at my broken nose and moaning like a baby. Jesus *Christ*, it hurts. My head's on fire . . . my nose, my mouth, my teeth . . . hot blood and tears streaming down my face . . .

"*FRED!*" I call out again through bloody lips.

And then I pass out.

Next thing I know Fred's standing over me with a burning cigarette lighter in his hand. Jenny is behind him. Their faces loom ghoulishly in the shadows of the flame.

"What are you doing down there?" says Fred.

"Bleeding," I tell him.

So that's it. We've got about a millimetre of water in the sink. No food, no plumbing, no light, no heat...

No, we've got heat. We've got a fire going in my room. Can you hear it crackling? Burning wood, table legs, paper... nice and hot. Enough light to see what we need to see.

"*Now* can we do something?" says Fred.

"We still don't know if He's gone."

"Of *course* He's fucking gone. The generator's packed in. The lift's stopped. We've got a fire going. He wouldn't let us have a fire, would He? If He was still here, He'd have put it out by now."

"Not necessarily. He could be—"

Fred slams his hand on the floor. "He's GONE, Linus! He's gone. Shit, man, what's the matter with you? He's gone. Why can't you *see* it?"

I look at Fred. "I don't know. I suppose I'm just scared."

He shakes his head. Angry, sad, kind. "There's nothing to be scared of now. He's gone."

"Yeah."

"Believe it. He's gone. We're on our own. No one's watching us any more. Now all we've got to do is get out."

All we've got to do is get out.

That was a few hours ago, maybe more than a few hours. A day, two days... who knows? I think Fred's right. I think He's gone. We've poked at the cameras, set light to them, spat at them... no reaction. He's gone. I don't know why I was so unwilling to accept it. Maybe I'm going mad. Stir crazy. Maybe I don't want to leave. Maybe I've got so used to being down here that the idea of getting out is even scarier than the idea of dying.

Or maybe it's something else.

Anyway, He's gone.

Dead?

Possibly.

Car crash, illness, accident, it could be anything. He fell down some stairs. He got a fish bone stuck in His throat. He drank too much, fell over, broke His neck. Stuck His finger in a wall socket and zapped Himself. These things happen, don't they? People die, nothing happens.

I mean, He's not likely to have many friends, is He? No one's going to miss Him. No one's going to come calling. And wherever we are, it's bound to be somewhere remote. He could be lying dead upstairs for years before anyone finds Him.

Then again, maybe I was right the first time. Maybe He's not dead, He's just gone. Got fed up with the whole thing. Got bored with it, got in his car and drove off to create another hell-hole somewhere else.

It's possible.

It's also irrelevant.

We've been trying to get out for hours, days, and we haven't got anywhere at all. We've hit things, bashed things, burned things, ripped things, hammered things, screamed at things. Nothing. Nowhere. We've sat down in the firelight and talked about things. Nothing. We've virtually burned the kitchen to the ground. Useless.

Worse than useless.

We forgot about the fridge.

I can't believe it. We forgot about the ice in the fridge. We set light to the kitchen...God knows why...it seemed like a good idea at the time...nearly fried ourselves in the process, and all we did was burn up the kitchen, ice and all. Got hot, got sweaty, got dry and tired, got thirsty...

We have half a cup of water left.

No days, no nights. No dates. Just times of sleep and non-sleep. The water's all gone. We lick condensation from the walls. Fred hammers at the lift door with whatever he can find. Saucepans, chair legs, bits of cooker. When they break he finds something else. The door is barely scratched.

Fred wipes sweat from his skin and sucks on the cloth.

"It's salt," I tell him. *Thalt*. My speech is thick and slurred. "It's just salt and stuff. It's no good."

He sniffs and rubs his throat. His lips are blue.

"There's a bottle of cleaning stuff in the bathroom," he says. "Bleach."

"It's liquid. Might be all right. We could do something—"

"It's *bleach*. It'll kill you."

He shrugs.

Jenny lies still. Her skin is ashen-grey, blotchy.

I stare at the fire and think of zebras.

Can't walk, can't get up. Can't speak. Mouth is foul. Tongue's as big as a mountain. Numb. Fred's stopped hammering. Sits cross-legged on the floor with his head bowed, like a Buddha in rags. Skin shrunk to his bones, eyes sunk inside his skull.

It hurts to pee.

Hurts to drink it.

Everything hurts.

Mountain . . . salt . . .
    I got it.
    Mountain . . . zebra.
    Dad's zebra.

> *On top of a mountain*
> *I saw a zebra*
> *eating some chips*
> *with his girlfriend called Debra.*
> *She didn't have salt*
> *and she didn't have sauce*
> *and she didn't have stripes*
> *because she was a horse*

Hey, Dad . . .
    Listen . . .
    I didn't mean anything, you know.
    I didn't mean to hurt you.
    OK?
    I'm sorry.

Fred's dead.

Went to the bathroom and drank the bleach.

Howled for an hour then coughed up blood and died.

So terrible. No words.

We can't get his body out of the bathroom. Too big. Doesn't matter. We don't go in there.

Jenny...

I had another vision thing. I saw her. She's lying beside me on the floor. The fire's going out. I can't get up to get any wood. I could burn you now. I could burn you now. I saw her, a long time ago. Looking up at the ceiling. Clear brown eyes, soft shiny hair, a curious little mouth.

He's a bad man, isn't he?

Looking up at the ceiling.

You're a bad man, Mister. A very bad man.

She's a feather of bones.

Long time.

Days.

A long way from everything. Floating, sad, cold. I wish things were different. I wish I was home. I wish Dad was sitting in his armchair with a cigarette and a glass of brandy, with a Wild West picturebook in his lap, with Mum in the kitchen, and the Monkees playing quietly on the CD player. I wish I was the little kid standing beside the chair, like a small ghost in blue flannelette pyjamas, giving off a silent fragrance of orange squash and skin. I wish I was standing there with my head cocked to one side, looking down at the pictures in the book. Pictures of cowboys, Buffalo Bill, Wild Bill Hickok, Wyatt Earp, Frank and Jesse James, Davy Crockett.

"He got a dog on his head."

Dad looks at me, then looks back at the picture of the handsome fellow in buckskin breeches and a raccoon-skin hat.

"That's Davy Crockett," he says.

"Doggett."

"Crockett, Davy Crockett. He was born on a mountain top in Mississippi—hang on, that's not right—somethingest state in the land of the free..." Dad sings quietly, "*Davy, Davy Crockett...*"

I point at Davy Crockett's hat. "Got a dog on his head."

"No, it's a raccoon. Ra-coon."

"Dog."

"Raccoon. It's a bit like a dog—"

"What dog?"

"It's not a dog, Linus. It's a raccoon. Ra-coon. Raccoon-skin hat. See its stripy tail?"

"It's past his bedtime," Mum says from the door.

"Raccoon dog," I say. "Bear. Fox."

Dad sighs, sips his brandy and turns the page.

"Come on, you," Mum says. "It's time for bed."

Jenny dies in my arms.
     Goes to sleep, doesn't wake up.
     My tears taste of blood.

Days, no light.
Hours days years.

.

flesh and blood meat drink that's all it isflesh and blood it's
allthesame chicken cow pig = 3 it's all just meatfleshfoodenergy
it's all the same turn the bad to good we're all animalsanimalsanimals
    meatanddrink
    your liquid eyes

so sorry
    so hurting skinned dry
    please forgive me

no tears now
    too long
    sick
    don'tcare the light the tunnel
    no

this is what i know
    it doesn't hurt any more
    this is